Tomes of Moreth

A Heist Forged by Fire and Lit by Desire

by

Brandy Stoker

Library of Congress: 2025925993

ISBN:

Paperback

978-1-969807-00-8

Hardcover

978-1-969807-01-5

Paperback Barnes

978-1-969807-02-2

Audiobook

978-1-969807-03-9

eBook

978-1-969807-04-6

General product safety regulation (GPSR)

This book complies with EU Regulation (EU) 2023/988 on general product safety.

Contact:

Brandy Jones/Brandy Over 40,

USA/Maryland, brandy@brandystoker.com

Tomes of Warning

This tale plunges headfirst into the tumultuous currents of human (and other) experience and contains themes that may be challenging for some readers.

I. Violence and Trauma

Intense Violence & War: Expect visceral depictions of violence and battle sequences that leave no doubt about their impact.

Gore/Injury: Injuries are sustained, and descriptions include significant bodily harm.

Loss and Grief: The specter of profound loss and grief looms large, including the death of key supporting characters.

Torture: Characters are subjected to, or threatened with, torture.

Childhood Trauma: The protagonist's background includes parental loss and childhood trauma related to claustrophobia and bullying.

II. Mature and Sexual Content

Complex Intimacies & Mature Themes: Relationships unfold with raw honesty, including sensual content between consenting adults.

Explicit Sexual Content: Includes explicit, detailed scenes involving themes of domination, spanking, restraint, & denial, infidelity, and non-monogamous situations (threesomes).

III. Dark and Disturbing Themes

Oppression/Slavery: The story includes references to an oppressive regime, human trafficking, and the use of slaves for violent training.

Morally Ambiguous Characters: Characters are killers, thieves, and operate within a morally grey resistance movement.

Cruelty and Mass Murder: Contains instances of extreme cruelty, including the intentional murder of civilians and children for tactical gain.

Substance Use: Includes depictions of alcohol consumption by characters.

Echoes of Aloria
Reading Order

Standalones:

Liberators of Media – Free Novella available on my website

- Dark Dystopian Fantasy
- Explains why the city of Media is protecting its citizens from people with magic.
- Note… This is going through rewriting currently for release in 2026.

Tomes of Moreth – A Standalone that would add flavor to any of the series. Why is the Order of Tamris after Will?

* **Aldrick and the Battle of Lumara** – A Standalone that offers the history of the War between Lumara and Mellryn.

* **Draco Mountains** – How do the dragons and the Dragon races fit into the world of Mordovia?

* **Story of Lady Anariel, Nar, and Khelek** – How did they meet and fall in love?

Series:

Escape from Media – The story of Malin and Will begins.

Journey to Aloria – They have escaped the city, but can they get to safety?

Welcome to Aloria – Available in June/July 2026. Order of Tamris

* **Book 4** – Will Explore the Elven Courts

* **Book 5** – We learn about Lumara and finish the series.

* Title is still in draft. I would love to know your thoughts.

Disclaimer

This is a work of fiction. All incidents and dialogue, and all characters, businesses, and locations are products of the author's imagination and are not to be construed as real. Any resemblance to person or persons living or dead is entirely coincidental.

To stay informed and be eligible for giveaways and sneak peeks of upcoming novels, go to brandystoker.com.
From here, you can sign up for my newsletter.
In return, you will get bonus materials.

DEDICATION

To the dark hearts and depraved minds who pick up this tome... not just for the magic and mayhem, but for the moments where the characters finally get down to business.

May your shadows be long, your desires be met, and your books glow just a little brighter when the good bits arrive.

You are my kind of unhinged, and I adore you for it.

For those that skip over those sections... I do still love you, too... but you are missing a piece of your soul.

Now, go forth and lust for more.

CONTENTS

TOMES of MORETH

CHAPTER 1 –
TROUBLE CALLS

Will Hawkson stared down the barrel of a mag-pistol in the piss-yellow light of a Talvi slum bar and wondered, not for the first time… whose husband was this? The stocky man's face was red as he fumbled with the weapon. His grimy appearance and the reek of stale fish suggested work in the food processing plant. Will tried to avoid situations like this. He always asked before things got physical. Sometimes the answer was the truth. Sometimes it wasn't.

Whose wife had he fucked this time?

The man shook in front of him, twitchy and furious, the pistol jerking with every tremor. The air thickened with sweat, sharp as vinegar. Between the overturned futon, the cracked windows leaking dusk, and the pungent stink of synth-onion takeout, Will almost laughed. The scene felt staged, like a cheap melodrama.

"You banged my wife. In my bed!" His voice wavered between a threat and a plea.

"I'm sorry," Will said, which was mostly true. He was always sorry, though rarely for the right reason.

He straightened, already anticipating the moment things would break loose, and studied the man's grip. The right thumb sat too high. The left index curled over the frame. Amateur. He sifted through the last couple of weeks of bad decisions and casual flings, but no wife surfaced.

"Who is your wife?" Will asked, still sorting through recent encounters. In a city built on forgettable distractions, she could have been anyone.

The man stepped closer, his boots squelching on the sticky floor.

"You don't even remember her, do you, you piece of shit? Tina remembered you and said your name last night while we were going at it."

Tina. Probably the buxom brunette from last week. Fun for an evening and instantly forgettable. If she hadn't made him say her name at the bar, it would already be gone.

"You have my sincerest apologies," Will said. "I do always ask if they're married first." He'd only been back in Media for a couple of months, and he kept his distractions brief.

"Shut it!" The man jabbed the gun toward him. Sweat dripped down his face, and he dragged his free hand across the back of his neck in a frantic swipe. "You people think you can just..."

Somewhere in the corridor, a door slammed and the windows rattled. The man flinched, eyes darting from the door back to Will. Nervous people lost control, and sometimes they never had any to begin with. With a tavern full of bodies, Will wasn't taking chances.

Will calculated the options. Two meters to the barred window. Less than one to the door. But the man would fire before he reached either. Talking was the only move left.

"If it helps, I'm between relationships," Will said, trying for calm he didn't feel. "So, it wasn't personal."

The man's nostrils flared. "I'm gonna end you. Men like you don't get to walk away." His finger twitched on and off the trigger. "Right here."

Will nodded, as if in solemn agreement. He couldn't really blame the husband. That was one of the many reasons he didn't bother with relationships. He willed his heartbeat to steady, but it beat a tattoo in his throat. He could have hurt the man, but it wasn't his fault his wife had fooled them both. He preferred to end this before there was any bloodshed, especially his own.

He needed a distraction. A break in the pattern. Something. Anything.

The man, his breath shaky, pulled the trigger.

Click.

The misfire bought Will a split second. He was already moving. He darted aside and knocked the gun from the husband's hand before a shot could be fired.

The misfire stunned the husband, but he recovered faster than Will expected. He lunged toward Will, shoulder slamming into his chest. The flimsy table gave way beneath them, splintering and sending overturned food containers flying.

As if the universe finally obliged, Will got his distraction. The tavern went still as a cold shadow filled the doorway. A seven-foot quarter-giant in a canvas greatcoat ducked inside.

Gorek. Of course.

The man who had saved him when he was a kid. He wasn't a kid anymore. The last thing Will needed was help with this. He had been avoiding Gorek for weeks, and here he was, towering in the doorway. Will cursed under his breath, wondering how the hell Gorek had even found him.

Half a second of distraction. That was all it took for the husband's wedding ring to smash into his jaw in a lucky left hook. The ring split skin as the punch landed, and blood flooded his mouth before he could react. It was sloppy form, but the ring made it count.

Will blocked the next flurry of punches but held back. The man didn't deserve real damage. His only crime was loving the wrong person. The blows slowed, each one weaker than the last, though maybe it gave the husband some sense of justice.

Then, from somewhere behind Will, a tavern patron slid the gun back across the floor.

Of course, someone gave the idiot his gun back.

The husband's eyes lit with renewed purpose, and he lifted the weapon like a club.

Will shifted to counter, but a massive hand closed around the husband's forearm before he could move.

Gorek. Of course.

He crushed down with a grip like a hydraulic vise and folded the mag-pistol in half, polymers squealing.

The husband let out a startled yelp, more shock than pain.

Subtlety had never been Gorek's talent.

The air seemed to shift as his shadow eclipsed them both.

"Enough," he said, his deep voice carrying through the quiet tavern.

Will hadn't heard Gorek speak in months, not since before his last transport job. He had forgotten how final Gorek's voice could sound, the same as when Will first met him at ten. Back then, everything felt imposing. Hard not to, after watching his family die at the city's hands.

They had argued before Will left, over his last Resistance job. It hadn't occurred to him that Gorek might have forgiven him.

Gorek hauled the man off the ground and dropped him onto the broken table. The husband went limp, terror hollowing his eyes. Will brushed debris off his black pants and pretended none of this was inconvenient.

Gorek's gaze traveled from Will's rumpled shirt to the blood on his face. Gorek didn't need words. The disappointment in his small, tight smile was enough.

"I didn't need your help," Will muttered, as the man bolted for the door.

"Maybe not. I expected to hear from you before the Resistance told me you were back in town, let alone that you have been here for over a month. They sent me to retrieve you for an assignment. Convenient timing."

He straightened the collar of his black linen shirt and brushed off a flake of dried blood he sincerely hoped wasn't his.

Gorek stood by the doorframe, waiting. His head nearly scraped the threshold as he paused for Will to go first.

Outside, the husband waited on the far side of the street with three other men, pointing and muttering. Will couldn't help himself. As he passed, he rubbed his jaw and gave the husband a thin, diplomatic smile.

"Let's call it even?"

The only response was a hissed curse in guttural street Talvish.

Will fell into step beside him. In the dim, crumbling passage, Gorek's size somehow made Will's six-foot-six frame feel small.

"Why did you step in? I could have handled it."

"Assignment's time sensitive," Gorek said. "Didn't feel like waitin' for chu to get hurt any more than needed." His footsteps were muffled, but still felt seismic beside Will.

The husband's curses faded behind, echoing like ghost static, as the stairwell swallowed them whole.

Evenings in Talvi meant cleaning time. The drones drenched the narrow walkways to combat disease, leaving a glistening scum that painted every alley in oil-slick iridescence. Gorek led with his shoulders hunched against the drizzle, head ducked so the overhangs didn't scrape his scalp. Will followed with his hands shoved deep in his jacket pockets, eyes already looking for trouble.

The slum footpaths were as treacherous as the people who used them. Blind corners, razor-spined gutters, and children in patched jumpsuits darted between trash bags and smoldering barrels. Gorek's bulk parted the crowd. People made way for him without thinking.

Gorek was known here as a protector, the kind of man who finished trouble. Not one who started it. A few people offered nervous half-bows. Others vanished into doorways, taking their secrets with them.

The hungry faces took him back to his childhood here, to that helpless, hollow feeling that used to swallow him whole. This place had cost him everything. It was why he joined the Resistance in the first place, to escape it and maybe give something back.

Gorek had been the one who showed him the path, the one who helped him turn his rage at the city into purpose. He never approved of the bloodier work Will took later, but he never tried to stop him either. He'd never given this place what it deserved in return. Maybe he never could.

Will had avoided the slums for most of the last decade. The free drinks at that tavern were the only reason he ever showed up. After tonight, he'd be lucky if they didn't spit in his drink.

Years of experience wouldn't let him relax. His mind ran through exits, movement patterns, and faces like a reflex. Four stood out. None mattered.

There was always the possibility that the city would have spies around, looking for the Resistance. Most of the time, that just meant more people to pay off in the slums, though.

He ticked off the faces he knew. The old guy with the rose tattoo on his neck was his usual fence. The twins ran message jobs for anyone paying cash. And the kid with the glass eye who'd once tried to pick his pocket and then spent a year shadowing him like a stray dog.

Will looked up. Gorek tugged his ear and stared straight ahead. Will knew the signal: move and shut up.

Will thought about asking him what he saw, but decided against it. Gorek's gift for silence was absolute. Some people filled the air with noise. Gorek made a vacuum.

They crossed a moss-slick bridge crowded with huddled bodies. Below, in the blackwater canal, feral dogs barked at runoff. The slum's smog filtered the sun into a jaundiced smear above the rooftops. Everything here was painted in layers of disappointment.

Will stepped into something soft and unpleasant and swore under his breath. Gorek shot him a sidelong look. The sting of embarrassment hit harder than it should have. At ten, it had been worse. He remembered scraping both knees bloody after falling on a staircase, fighting tears while Gorek picked him up and told him to "move forward." Will knew he wasn't that kid anymore, and Gorek wasn't just the man who'd saved him. He was the closest thing to a father he'd ever had. The realization dug under his ribs, carrying guilt he didn't want to examine.

The memory lingered, equal parts shame and gratitude. Will wondered if he'd ever made Gorek proud, or if the big man even believed in pride at all, aside from treating it like a liability.

They turned onto Lattice Row, where the city's most stubborn lowlifes lingered and the Resistance's worst-kept secrets circulated in whispers. Will's skin prickled. He counted seven new faces in the last block, all loitering. Some might have been allies. Most probably weren't.

Looking up, he caught sight of the wooden sign. A landmark that had hung here for centuries, even before the city was freed from slavery. To most of the city, Stoneholds was known as a mercantile shop selling non-magical goods from across Mordovia.

To a stranger, Stoneholds looked like any other hole-in-the-wall shop: bolts of cloth in the windows, sacks of flour and eggs stacked by the door, faded letters promising "Custom Repairs" and "Linen Restitch."

Stoneholds stayed profitable enough that Gorek could bribe the right officials.

Will's attention caught on the tiny runes carved into the doorframe, each sigil shimmering with restrained energy. They marked the entry as watched and warded. The symbols were older than Elven script, older than recorded history. Their looping strokes sat somewhere between ornament and language.

A familiar static buzzed in the air, tugging at muscle memory. Home. His fingers twitched with anticipation. The glamour hid the magical inventory from anyone without magic. To most, this was just another store.

Gorek waited for a woman in a pink scarf to limp out, then guided Will to the side door, which was little more than a dented panel with a rusted knob. Gorek tapped a pattern on the frame. Something inside clicked and chittered before unlocking.

Will slipped inside after him.

"I should have reached out." Will exhaled. "I know you were angry about the Judge assignment. The

Resistance wanted me to hand off the money and walk. I killed him instead… and I still think I had good reason."

Gorek's jaw worked. "I'm glad he's dead. I never liked him. But chu were given an assignment for a reason. We needed him alive. Chu are rash. I taught chu better."

The frustrated shake of the big guy's head hurt more than the words.

"Someone knew what they were doing when they gave me that assignment," Will said, his jaw tight. "They wanted me to walk in on that, and they knew what I'd do."

"But that was over a year ago," Gorek muttered. "Lysa's still mad at me for blowing up at chu."

He'd promised himself, last time, that he wouldn't come back.

So much for keeping promises.

Gorek still wouldn't meet his eyes, like he'd known all along Will would never stay gone.

The door opened into darkness. Another magical barrier Will knew about. Gorek ducked inside, and Will followed, tension settling across his shoulders like an old coat.

Inside smelled of wet wool and ozone, and the low hum of surveillance cameras vibrated in the walls. Gorek moved silently despite his size. Will matched his steps without thinking, muscle memory kicking in.

They passed through a long hallway lined with bins of fabric, past a counter stacked with ledgers and bills. Although it looked like nobody manned the front, there were plenty of eyes upon it.

"Lysa will clock me if ya don't see her," Gorek muttered. "Ye know dat woman I married ain't forgivin'. She still mad since ya left."

Will winced. Avoiding Gorek meant avoiding her, too. "I'll see her," he said quietly.

Gorek herded him through Stoneholds' inner corridors like a sheepdog steering a particularly problematic lamb. Will followed, winding through low ceilings and storerooms until the city noise faded behind triple-layered walls.

They stepped through the gelatinous portal into the secure safehouse. The shift was immediate with no technology. Only glowing crystals for light and a thick smell of ozone. The change brought back bittersweet memories.

The portal opened into a narrow tunnel lined with doors.

At the end of the hall stood a steel door secured with three locks. Gorek knocked once, and it slid open along a hidden seam.

A thin, bony silhouette waited on the other side. Will recognized Willa instantly. She was slim, bony, twitchy, with a streak of repressed violence. She had been working with the Resistance for a while. She stepped aside, wordless, and let them enter.

Will had grown up here after the city murdered his family. It wasn't just familiar. It was everything. It was home.

The walls were cluttered with annotated street maps, all with colored pins and markers. There were stacks of folders in uneven piles. At the center stood a worn war table crowded with mugs, discarded food cartons, and a handgun stripped to its bones.

Even here, in the safest place the Resistance had, Will scanned for exits and threats. Old habits. Old scars. He hated how automatic it was.

Then he caught Gorek doing the same, and the knot in his chest loosened just a little.

He reached for the coffee pot, but Gorek's hand clamped down on his shoulder. The quarter-giant guided him sideways and dropped him into a battered office chair. The springs groaned in protest.

"Wait." Gorek moved to the reinforced door and planted himself there, arms folded.

So, Will waited. Gorek never minded silence, but this felt colder than usual. His gut told him to find Lysa, but he stayed put. Gorek told him to wait. That was enough.

He'd missed this more than he cared to admit.

The girl who'd let them in silently handed Will a mug of tea and retreated into the shadows. Gorek left a moment later, wearing the same disapproving expression that always made Will feel twelve again.

He wrapped both hands around the cup and savored the burn. Slowly, his shoulders loosened. He slouched, took another sip, and tried to ignore the faint tremor in his fingers.

Still on guard, he was home. Or as close as he'd get.

Five minutes passed. Maybe ten. Long enough for his pulse to steady and the adrenaline to fade into its usual dull hum. Someone had left a candy wrapper on the war table. He flicked it away and forced himself not to fidget.

The inner door opened, and Angel walked in. Technically, she was Angelina, but she'd punched the "ina" out of her life years ago.

She looked just as good as he remembered. Maybe better. She wore a matte-black tactical jacket and gray slacks. Her boots were polished to a mirrored shine. The short boy-cut was new... a bit edgier than he remembered. It made her blue eyes look like weapons. A scar split along her jaw and caught the light like a blade.

She didn't smile. With their history, he didn't expect her to. Still... he hoped.

He met Angel in high school. He killed for the first time that same year. They had been on and off back then, but times changed. So did they. Both became killers for the Resistance. She stayed and moved into leadership. He left.

She was one of the few who ever turned him down. That made her impossible to forget.

"Will," she said evenly.

He gave a lazy, seated salute. "Angel... or should I say Lieutenant," he said, deliberately flippant.

Her jaw tightened as she looked him over with the same expression someone gives a cockroach they can't kill but are forced to tolerate.

"The prodigal son returns. It pisses me off how you get all the sweet assignments. Why they sent you for the Fellspire Citadel retrieval, I will never understand."

She paused, then added, "How long has it been?"

He shrugged. "Not long enough to miss the sound of your voice."

It was a lie. He had missed her, and it irked him more than he liked.

Angel rolled her eyes, though something shifted in her posture. Amusement, maybe. Or just muscle memory.

She crossed to the table, picked up the disassembled pistol, and began putting it back together as she spoke.

"Orders came down that you're needed for a high-priority transport. No drama. No improvising. Just deliver to Aloria. You should be grateful for the chance to get out of the city. I know you never liked it here."

Will wondered what else she remembered. He remembered the little sound she made right before she came.

"I hadn't planned on taking a job. I had this wild idea I might take a break."

She ignored him. "Client is at Cistern Row near the old waterworks. Codename Pixie. You won't be able to miss her. And once again, you are to drop her off and stay away."

Will searched his internal roster. Pixie. Nothing.

Gorek walked back in. His eyes trained on Will.

Angel snapped the pistol together and set it down, the metal clacking sharply. "You'll go in as a courier. No heroics. The Resistance needs her out of the city, and we agreed to get her to a safe place."

He hadn't planned on taking an assignment, but the itch was already there. His ledger was still too far in the red. After the last assignment, and the way he'd left things with the Resistance, he never expected them to call him back.

Trouble sounded like fun and a chance to help others.

"Don't fuck it up," Angel added, voice sharp enough to cut.

"When have I ever fucked it up?" Will asked.

Gorek gave a low grunt. That was answer enough.

"We've run more missions together than most. I have seen you fuck up more times than I can count," she assured.

"Those were my early years. We both fucked up regularly. We haven't worked together in a long time. Last time, they told me it was a quick Judge payoff. Then, I walked in on him assaulting that woman. I was justified in killing him. I couldn't have known she was his wife, and even if I had, it wouldn't have made it right. I don't want surprises this time." Will leveled his eyes at her.

"You did right in my eyes, but it wasn't my call. I follow orders. That is the difference between us."

"Leadership wanted the payoff. Apparently, this assignment is an olive branch." Angel straightened and held his gaze before handing him a folder. "It is in the Resistance's best interest for her to get out of the city, and she's trouble... needs to be taken out of the city before there is trouble. She has a habit of starting fires... literal ones. Don't..." She paused, searching for the right words. "I know you. Don't make her yours to fix."

The words hit harder than she likely intended. His stomach shifted. He forced a crooked smile.

"Since when do I follow standard Resistance procedures?"

Angel smiled then, brief and sharp, with just a flash of teeth, but the air crackled between them. There had always been electricity with her... sometimes literal with her static magic. It made their old partnership both so effective and such a disaster. "Don't come crawling back when things go sideways if you ignore me."

He'd forgotten how much he liked that sharp, lopsided grin.

Will considered saying something, but he knew Gorek was watching. He stood, rolled his shoulders, and closed the folder.

Angel's voice stopped him halfway to the door.

"Remember. I'm saying this twice because you have a thick skull. Don't fuck up. And don't get attached."

He looked back. "If I do, I'll report directly back to you, so you can be the first to know," he said with a roll of his eyes. Then to Gorek. "Can you please let Lysa know I was here, and I wanted to see her... but Resistance business dragged me away? Please let her know that this Pixie I'm picking up, and I, will be coming to visit."

"Aye, she will appreciate seeing ya."

Will left the safehouse. Gorek's shadow trailed him through the corridors.

Will drew in a slow breath, squared his shoulders, and started toward Cistern Row.

Back in the game. As if he ever really left.

Chapter 2 – Pixie

William spotted a petite woman with her back to him, with the sunset highlighting her form like a spotlight. It had to be his contact, 'Pixie.' She fit the name. Barely five feet tall, slender as a willow branch.

Her hair blazed fire-red in the fading light, cascading in wild waves over her shoulders, seeming to move with a life of their own. One look at those curves and that defiant hip told him there were plenty of enjoyable ways to get close.

Standing alone in Cistern Row meant she could either... hold her own or she had a reckless streak.

Maybe both.

She turned with fluid grace, and Will's breath caught.

She was beautiful, yes, but that was not what struck him first. It was her brazenness. A perfect sphere of flame spun lazily between her fingers, no larger than a marble but burning with impossible intensity. The light danced across her heart-shaped face, casting shifting shadows and turning her eyes into molten sunset.

She toyed with the flame in broad daylight... in a city where magic users were hunted like vermin. Will scanned the empty alley, the boarded windows, and the distant pulse of the market several streets away. No immediate observers.

His pulse lifted.

Some dangers came with a warning.

Some invited you in.

She looked like both.

It was brazen and made the hair on his neck rise. In the Talvi slums, walls had eyes and shadows had memories.

Will cleared his throat.

"Pixie, I presume?" His tone stayed even, though the casual display of magic gnawed at his nerves.

The flame disappeared between her fingers as she lifted her gaze to him. Her expression shifted, turning from idle curiosity into something hungry. Her smile curled slowly and intentionally, sharp enough to feel like a dare.

"Yum," she purred, her accent polished and unmistakably Media aristocracy. Her gaze dragged up his frame from boots to face, lingering too long to be polite.

"They told me to expect Hawk," she said, stalking toward him, her boots tapping a confident rhythm on the stone. Not hurried. Not hesitant. Close enough to taste the trouble.

He lifted a hand to halt her approach, more formality than conviction, and she ignored it without hesitation. Her fingers traced a slow line along his forearm, drifting to his palm as if sampling him, testing boundaries he hadn't agreed to but was in no hurry to enforce.

"They failed to mention you'd be a tree I'd like to climb."

Cinnamon and smoke clung to her, wrapping around him like a warm hand at the base of his spine.

Will bit back a grin, not because she left him unaffected, but because appearing indifferent was part of his game. Angel's warning flickered at the edge of his thoughts, and he dismissed it just as quickly. Following orders had never been one of his talents.

He could understand why Angel had cautioned him, but caution had never tasted nearly as tempting as this trouble. And this fiery little contact radiated trouble wrapped in temptation. Fun had been in short supply lately, and Pixie looked like the kind he wouldn't mind getting burned by.

"So, how long do I get to keep you?" Her smile widened as if she already knew the answer.

Will let the question sit there, warm and suggestive, then chose the professional answer, or at least the version of it he could manage right now.

"I've been tasked with getting you out of the city and to Aloria. Travel time depends on conditions, but a month is reasonable."

A month with her would either be entertaining or a disaster. Possibly both.

His gaze flicked briefly across her low neckline before shifting past her shoulder to the far end of the alley. Still quiet. Still too quiet. No visible movement ever meant safety in Talvi.

They needed to get moving.

Focus first. Temptation later.

Will watched her hands. It was instinct. Carved into him long before training. In the slums, you watched hands first. Hands told you what someone meant to take. Her fingers were elegant, practiced, and marked with faint pale scars trailing along her knuckles and forearms. Not decorative. Earned. There was history carved into her skin, and none of it looked gentle.

"I can see subtlety is not your strong suit," he said quietly.

She laughed. Not polite. Not nervous. A full-bodied, unapologetic burst loud enough to startle a cluster of birds from a nearby rooftop. She didn't flinch when they took off. She just watched them go, amused.

Her eyes glittered with something too close to a challenge.

"Tell me something, Pet. Ever been with a fire-caster?"

The question hung between them, warm and daring.

"Not yet." His answer made her smile sharpen.

He let the moment linger, then shifted back to business.

"But before we find out how dangerous that can get, we need to move. That your only bag?" He nodded toward the oversized duffel at her feet. It looked almost comically large against her frame.

"Yes," she said, watching him closely.

Will didn't ask. He just reached down, lifted the bag with one hand, and swung it over his shoulder like it weighed nothing.

The sound she made in response was half gasp, half approval.

They walked.

The alley funneled into a narrow corridor of rusted pipes and broken brick, far enough from the market noise that footsteps sounded louder than they should. The city swallowed sound here, turned every echo into something watched, even when nothing moved.

Pixie stayed close beside him, not clinging, just brushing the edge of his space like she was testing invisible boundaries. At first, she tried looping her arm through his. The height difference made it awkward. After one irritated breath, she let her hand drop and pretended she never tried.

He pretended not to notice.

"So," she murmured, voice dipped in smoke and velvet confidence, "do I call you Hawk the entire time, or do you actually have a name?"

"Will. Will Hawkson."

She repeated it, slow, like she was tasting it.

"Will."

A faint grin curved her mouth. "Short for willpower? Because you're already testing mine."

His pulse kicked once. Only once.

He kept his stride steady.

She waited a beat before offering, casually, "My name is Lydia."

Just Lydia. No family name. No House. No title.

People gave only a single name when they had something to hide, something to sell, or nothing left to claim. He didn't know which one she was. Yet.

He filed it away with the scars on her hands and the flames she'd spun between her fingers.

Will led the way through the dilapidated streets of Talvi, Lydia still beside him. He checked on her occasionally and caught the disdain tightening her expression. Her designer clothes and perfectly styled hair stood out like a slap against the poverty around them.

Will's jaw tightened, the muscle in his cheek jumping beneath his skin as she muttered "filthy little street rat" under her breath at yet another passing child.

His fingers curled into his palm, nails biting crescents into his skin. He quickened his pace, making her work to keep up.

Finally, he couldn't listen anymore. "They didn't choose this," he said, voice low enough only she could hear. "People here survive how they can. Hunger doesn't give many options."

For a heartbeat, she looked like she might snap.

Instead, something flickered across her expression. Raw. Unguarded. Almost wounded.

Then it vanished beneath sharp arrogance.

"I know that life," she said. Her voice was quieter now, without the dramatic flare she'd worn like armor. "I just refused to stay in it. I fought and fucked my way out while others just accepted their fate. Don't romanticize suffering, Pet. Others... get comfortable in their cages."

Will stopped walking and let her pass him.

"I realize you have opinions," he said, tone steady but edged, "but don't talk like that around me again. Or I'll leave you here, and the Resistance can send someone else to get you out."

She blinked once.

Silence stretched between them.

Will let it linger.

Someone needed to stand up for them. Even if they couldn't hear her words, he had. And he would not tolerate anyone, especially someone like her, talking about these people like they were already broken. They were survivors. People like him. People who clawed their way through life with whatever was left. They didn't deserve her careless cruelty... especially the children.

As the alley forced her to walk ahead of him, he had ample opportunity to eye the way her whole body moved from side to side as she walked. Each step was a deliberate stroke, her form tracing a lazy figure-eight that made the gritty street feel like a velvet runway.

If she kept walking like that, the month to Aloria might actually be tolerable.

"I'm sorry for my words," she said eventually. "We can change topics. I do see the potential for a rather... delightful trip."

"It's a long way to Aloria. You might get tired of me before we even clear the city gates."

She scoffed and flicked a strand of scarlet hair over her shoulder, revealing the delicate line of her throat and the faint bruise of a hickey.

"Variation is the key to enjoyment. The Chancellor taught me that."

He let her take the lead. With a few steps between them, her sway shifted from casual to calculated, a slow hypnotic dare that seemed impossible with a skirt that tight.

"Chancellor?"

"They should have told you I'm a priority," she said, voice lowering to something velvet and private. "I belong to Malven Ramie. Chancellor of the Entertainment District. I warmed his bed, and the beds of his favorites, and while they used me, I collected their secrets. Names, dates, transactions, alliances, betrayals. Enough to bury half the Council."

She looked over her shoulder, eyes glinting with manic pride.

"When one of his orgies spiraled into chaos, someone caught me using my flames... They can add so much pleasure to the evening, but people panic when they remember it can also destroy. You'll see," she said.

"So now he has a choice. Get me out of the city or watch me release every secret I've stored in that vault and send his whole empire screaming into ash."

Will drew a slow breath. "That part was not in your file." His jaw tightened. He wondered if Angel had left it out intentionally. "It must have been an oversight."

She smirked. "Files rarely tell the truth. Especially when the men with power are the ones writing them."

"Oh. And one more treat. Malven can read minds. The Council does not know. Imagine the chaos if the liars discovered they were being watched. Now that the Resistance knows, he can stay in office as long as he plays by their rules."

She winked as if she'd handed him a weapon.

Maybe she had.

They continued through the winding back routes of Talvi. The deeper they went, the narrower the streets became until the alleys felt less like roads and more like veins carrying them toward the city's hidden heart.

Will stopped in front of a narrow passage where crumbling brick walls leaned inward. The air was damp, and rust-colored puddles reflected the fading light.

"I need to blindfold you," he said. "Fewer people who know this route keep it safer, and I'm not taking you to the typical safe house."

Lydia's crimson lips curled into a mischievous smile as she pressed against his chest. Her delicate fingers slid beneath his leather vest to trace circles around his nipples.

"Mmm. I do love a man with a blindfold and initiative. I doubt this is the ending I'm hoping for, but maybe we can try again tonight," she purred. Her fiery hair caught the light as she tilted her head back to look up at him. "Just promise you'll hold me close, Pet. I want to feel every... single... heartbeat."

A soft purr rolled up her throat.

Will ignored the heat crawling up his spine and tied the blindfold securely over her eyes.

She sighed in contentment.

He lifted her without effort. Her body molded easily over his shoulder, equal parts weight and intention.

Water dripped somewhere ahead, echoing through the stone like distant, stalking footsteps, entering the same path he had been on earlier. Ahead, the magical barrier shimmered, shifting like liquefied glass.

"This part will not feel good," he warned. "We need to go through a protective barrier that keeps those without magic out. It will not feel good, especially your first time through. It will feel like drowning for a moment. Do not fight it."

He paused, wondering if he should warn her about the nausea that followed, or if that would only make her more difficult. He felt her squirm in his arms, trying to get out. She was too late anyway.

He stepped through.

The barrier swallowed them whole.

On the other side of the portal, the air was warmer. The walls hummed faintly with protective spells and ozone. Will's steps slowed as they approached Lysa's door.

His pulse quickened, wondering how Lysandra, the woman who had been like a mother to him since childhood, would react to his return. Especially given how poorly they parted ways.

CHAPTER 3 –
FAMILY MATTERS

Walking through the front door, felt like transporting himself back in time. The scent of hearth fire and herbs drifted from deeper inside, from the Burrow that Gorek and Lysa made their home. It was the one they had invited him to make his home.

Will shifted Lydia's weight and hesitated.

He had not seen her in over a year, and he had arrived with trouble slung over his shoulder.

Will knew the volatility of her fire magic meant he needed to contain her in the safest, most magically guarded space possible. Gorek had told him that she wanted to see him. Will had told him to warn her that he was coming with this person. He had taken steps to ensure she didn't know where they were. Surely, she would not be too upset about that, but how should she be about his disappearance for so long?

Opening the door revealed the entry room unchanged since his childhood. Familiar cooking sounds echoed from the kitchen down the hall. For a moment, he considered turning around, sparing Lysa this intrusion.

Instead, he carried Lydia down the hallway, past his own bedroom. He knew he didn't want to share that with this stranger.

Will hesitated in the doorway to the smaller guest room, just past his room. It had seen its share of visitors, but this would have been the first woman he brought. The room was dim and unadorned, but the bed was large and comfortable.

Lysa kept a tidy home, so the clean linens and rugs were of decent quality, not too showy, but better than the threadbare sheets he had seen in other safe houses.

He set her bag down first, then closed the door with his foot. He slowly released her, letting her body slide against his till her feet hit the floor. Her hands questing boldly on his arms, then chest, before roaming lower. He stepped back when her feet were solid below her; their height difference felt monumental. He caught her wrists to still them as she moved to raise the blindfold.

He was not looking forward to hearing a comment or insult from someone who would likely turn her nose up at her surroundings. To him, this place was happiness, or at least all he knew of it. Her hands roamed, and she teasingly ground herself against him.

He said, "I would like to explore more of this, but I need to verify if we will be staying or not. You will be on your best behavior... if we do stay," he cautioned.

He helped lift the blindfold off her head, and her hands began smoothing her fiery locks, as her eyes surveyed the room. He steeled himself for an expected jab about the sparseness of the room.

"Not as squalid as I expected," she said, smoothing her skirt and glancing around. "Cozy, even. They had cautioned me that my safe houses would not be much to speak of."

He held her gaze, then softened his tone. "You'll stay here, out of sight. No wandering. No noise. No fire. You understand?"

She leaned back on her hands, eyes gleaming, and crossed her legs with slow, theatrical precision. "You want me to play the docile waif, Pet?" she purred, her voice slipping back into the smoky register that almost convinced him she could behave. "What do I get if I'm a good girl?"

His hand found her chin, tilting her face and leaning down until her lips nearly brushed his. "I have quite a few thoughts on how you will be rewarded for your behavior. I feel like it would benefit you to learn quickly how good things can be for you if you listen.

We can call what will happen later... obedience training."

"What if I want to be a bad girl?" she asked as she drew his hand to her breast, which he realized was uncorseted.

"We will cover both sides to be sure," he assured, flicking her nipple with his fingers. For a heartbeat, neither of them moved. Lydia's eyes searched his, hunting for a crack in his resolve, but Will stayed cold.

After a moment, she relented, feigning disappointment. "Fine," she said, folding her arms. "But you'll owe me. I'm a woman who likes her debts collected, Pet."

"I won't be long," Will growled, eliciting a giggle of pleasure from her as he stepped away.

Then he left her to get comfortable, heading to the kitchen to greet Lysa. The scent of stewed lamb and fresh-baked honey cookies wafted through the air, mingling with the musty aroma of the ancient oak furniture that had survived more generations of Talvian winters than he knew.

Lavender sachets hung from copper hooks along the hallway, their delicate perfume cutting through the heaviness of the cooking smells, transporting Will back to nights when he'd fallen asleep to that same comforting blend.

The moment Will rounded the worn pine threshold into the kitchen, the radiant heat of the cast-iron stove washed over him like a warm tide. The stove's blackened surface glowed where embers still smoldered beneath its belly, sending coppery warmth rolling into every corner. Lysa stood at its side, her silhouette etched by the amber flicker of the cooking fire. Her long braid was streaked silver, the color of moonlight, and swung between her shoulder blades as she guided a sturdy wooden spoon through a bubbling, aromatic stew. Each scrape of spoon against pot sounded in time with her steady breath, a soft percussion in the otherwise hushed room.

Will's heavy boot creaked on the third floorboard, the one he always promised he'd repair. The familiar betrayal of wood on leather made him wince.

In an instant, Lysa pivoted with the grace of a dancer, despite the sixty winters etched into her skin. The gleam of a filleting knife appeared in her weathered hand, its blade catching the flames' glow. Her eyes, the green of freshly cut emeralds marred only by fine lines at the corners, softened when they landed on him.

"Going to run your favorite taste tester through?" Will asked with a grin, lifting his hands in mock-exasperation.

The knife clattered to the counter as Lysa dropped her arms and stepped forward into his embrace. Her cotton apron, faded to dove gray, carried the scent of crushed rosemary and decades of kitchen triumphs. Her Talvian accent was not nearly as thick as Gorek's, but it was equally rich and slow as molasses. Hearing it again, it wrapped around him like a second hug.

"Gorek said you'd be coming, but I didn't expect you so soon," she murmured, her voice mingling with the stew's rising steam. "The spirits must have whispered for me to prepare your favorite stew. The one with lamb, root vegetables, and burnt sage."

Will swallowed. His throat felt constricted by the memory of the promise he'd made here long ago... that he would never lie to her. "I wanted to make it back sooner..." The words tasted sour on his tongue. He'd said the same thing before he left a year ago.

Lysa waved a calloused hand, brushing aside his apology like a wisp of smoke. "What matters is you're here now." Her gaze flicked toward the dim hallway beyond the kitchen arch. "Though you aren't alone, I hear."

He shifted his weight on the creaky floorboards. "I did bring some Resistance work," he confessed, studying the deep grain and one of his childhood carvings still etched where his small blade had nicked the edge.

"I heard," she said, her lips tightening. "As long as she behaves... I won't tolerate any high-and-mighty airs undoing what we've built here." The steel in her tone reminded Will of every scrap of her survival instinct, honed in a world that devoured the weak.

With a gentle motion, Lysa pulled out the wooden chair opposite her with its back splintered in two places. She sat, folding her hands on the scarred tabletop like a judge awaiting testimony. "Tell me what's been happening."

Will offered the polished version of events, aware she already knew more than she let on, thanks to her far-reaching network of informants. When at last she nodded, he felt her attention sharpen.

She leaned forward, "Where do you see yourself going from here, boy?" He traced the shallow notch with his thumb.

"I've spent too many nights killing and stealing for the Resistance. I want... to try something different. I need more."

"But you took this assignment for them," she observed, an eyebrow rising like a question mark.

"Angel asked." He forced a nonchalant shrug.

"Ahh, yes. I know how you feel about Angel. She's a good one. Strong and fierce. A strong match with you."

"She's married to the job. That's who she is, and I can't be that with her. The job is interesting. It keeps me going, but... It can't be everything... like it is for her."

Lysa's laugh was the dry crackle of kindling. "You're right. You would hate that. You always had a free spirit. I've called on the Oracles for you, and I know happiness will find you. Just trust. As far as the Resistance, they know their operatives." She reached out, her fingers brushing his hand—thin, papery skin against his calluses.

"I've heard of this Pixie," she added, voice softening. "Don't let yourself get too tangled, but I won't forbid it. That'd only drive you deeper."

Will's mouth opened, then closed, recalling his number one rule: never lie to Lysa. She could strip away falsehoods as easily as one reads the weather in a restless sky.

He cleared his throat. "Her name is Lydia. We'll be in the guest room next to mine. I need to help her settle in... to go over some details. We'll join you for dinner afterward. Is seven o'clock good?" The half-truth hovered between them like a stray wisp of smoke. It was neither a full confession nor an outright lie.

Lysa's lips twitched upward. "Settling in, is it?" She brushed invisible dust from her apron. "Gorek returns in an hour. That should be perfect timing."

She rose, and as Will followed, he felt the familiar swell of protectiveness in her arms. Will breathed in the familiar scent of rosemary and woodsmoke, memories flooding him.

He stood taller now, yet her embrace still felt like home. He recalled her help with skinned knees bandaged with gentle hands, stern lectures about schoolwork, a childhood cobbled together from whatever normalcy Lysa could salvage for him. She had fought like a dog to ensure that he went to school... even college. When she finally released him, he walked back toward Lydia with lighter steps, as if Lysa's blessing... reluctant though it might be... had absolved him for his poor behavior.

The hallway back to the guest room felt shorter than before, as if memory had folded the space inward. The lavender sachets brushed gently against his shoulder as he passed, releasing a faint cloud of scent that settled his pulse into something calmer, steadier.

Calm he would need.

He hesitated outside the door. Part of him hoped she slept. Another part hoped she waited awake. Neither part wanted to admit which one was stronger.

Will opened the door and was met with the sight of Lydia, lying naked. Her skin glistened with a thin layer of sweat. Her pale skin stood out against the dark sheets, and her hair fanned out across the pillow. One breast was exposed, her nipple hardened from her ministrations. Her leg was bent at the knee, giving a glimpse of the curve of her hip and the smooth skin of her thigh. Her hand moved between her legs, stopping when he moved inside the room and closed the door. She looked devilish, and his thoughts moved to all the things he wanted to do with that tiny body. His smile grew as he realized he would likely experience all the thoughts and more.

"I couldn't wait," she murmured, her voice low and husky. "I had to start without you." She withdrew her fingers from between her legs, the tips glistening with her arousal. Slowly, deliberately, she raised them to her mouth, sucking each one clean, her tongue swirling around the digits, tasting her own excitement.

He watched her intently, his breath hitching each time her lips wrapped around her fingers, simulating the act that had been consuming his thoughts. He could imagine that those lips would look amazing wrapped around him, while she was looking up. She held his gaze, her cheeks flushed, her breasts rising and falling with each anticipatory breath as she sat up, allowing the sheet to slide down her body, revealing her nakedness. She crooked her finger toward him, a silent command to join her by the bed.

He moved forward, as if in a trance, his cock hardening with each step. When he reached the bed, she leaned forward, her hands reaching for his belt. She unbuckled it slowly, her fingers brushing against his skin, sending jolts of electricity through him. She unbuttoned his pants, her knuckles grazing his erection as she unfastened each button until he sprang from the confinement, earning him an audible gasp. He let out a low groan, his body aching with desire.

She looked up at him; her eyes filled with lust as she pulled down his pants. He kicked off his shoes and stepped out of the offensive clothing. He was hard and ready, just inches from her face.

She gasped softly, her breath hot against his shaft, as she licked her lips. "You're so hard," she murmured, her fingers wrapping around him, stroking him gently.

His vest and shirt followed quickly, leaving him naked as she was. She ran her hands over his chest, his stomach, her nails scratching lightly over his skin. He shivered, his cock throbbing in her hand. She leaned forward, her tongue flicking out against the tip of his cock, licking away the bead of pre-cum that had formed there. He gasped, his hips jerking forward slightly.

As if she had been reading his mind earlier, she looked up at him, her eyes locked onto his as she slowly parted her lips and guided his stiff cock into her mouth. He let out a low, guttural groan, the warmth and wetness of her mouth engulfing the head of his cock, sending electric jolts of pleasure coursing through his nerves. She applied suction, her cheeks concaving as she began to bob her head up and down, taking more of his shaft into her mouth with each descent. Her hand wrapped around the base of his cock, twisting and stroking him in sync with the rhythm of her mouth. Her tongue swirled around the sensitive underside of his shaft, tracing the thick vein that pulsed with his heartbeat.

The sudden heat of her magic seared his inner thigh, the sharp, acrid scent of singed hair and flesh filling his nostrils. He reacted instantly, tangling his fist in her hair and pulling her off him. "No," he growled, his voice thick with a mix of pain and arousal. "Do you want to see what I do to bad girls?"

She looked up at him, her eyes hooded with desire, a seductive smile playing on her lips. "Yes," she purred, her tongue darting out, wetting her lower lip.

Seeing the need to take control, he lifted her effortlessly and threw her over his knee. He shifted his position, raising his hand to spank her. "You want this?" He wasn't interested in causing her genuine harm; the threat of domination was his true aim. His palm hovered over her bare ass, waiting.

"Yes, Pet," she cooed, arching her back to present herself to him, her ass pushing up against his hand. He hid his surprise at her eager response, realizing he would have to think of a more creative punishment.

He moved her again, maneuvering her as if she weighed nothing, positioning her at the edge of the bed with her legs dangling over the side and her ass in the air. It was then that he saw her glistening opening, wet and ready for him. He decided exactly what would pleasure him the most at that moment.

"Someone needs to learn to behave. I said no fire," he warned.

"You'll see my flames can be so pleasurable."

Under normal circumstances, he would have slowly entered her, easing his way in inch by inch. But this was a punishment, after all. He guided his cock to her entrance, then thrust deep inside her with one forceful motion. The tightness around him was almost magical. He felt his cockhead hit a wall and pushed even deeper, holding himself fully sheathed within her tight, wet heat. She groaned, her body tensing beneath him as she winced from the sudden intrusion. Her fingers clutched at the sheets, knuckles turning white as she gasped for breath.

"Maybe I'll have to be bad more often," she whispered, arching her hips to meet his, feeling him sink deeper into her.

Her words drew a low, primal growl from him, a sound he hadn't expected. He could feel her tightness clenching around his cock, the sensation sending waves of pleasure through him. He withdrew almost entirely, feeling her grip him as if reluctant to let him go, then thrust back in, filling her completely. He repeated the motion, building a steady rhythm, the slap of their flesh meeting echoing in the room.

Not wanting to reach his climax too soon, he pulled out, his cock glistening with her wetness. He looked down at her, flushed and breathless, her breasts heaving with each panting breath. He had coaxed at least two orgasms from her already, her body shuddering beneath him each time. He could see the effect he had on her when he turned her over to see her nipples hard and peaked, her skin damp with sweat. He reached down, his thumb finding her clit, circling the sensitive bundle of nerves as he watched her squirm and gasp beneath him.

"Maybe my best punishment will be not letting you come," he teased, his voice hoarse with passion. He slid his fingers between her legs, tracing the wetness of her labia, circling her clit with a touch as light as a feather. She bucked her hips, eager for more, but he pulled back, a wicked grin on his face.

He entered her slowly, inch by thick inch, feeling her stretch around him. She gasped, nails digging into his back, trying to pull him deeper. But he held back, keeping his pace torturously slow. He watched as her cheeks flushed, her breath hitched, and her body trembled on the brink of orgasm. Then he stopped, pulling out completely, leaving her empty and aching.

He slipped a finger inside her, curling it to hit the spot that made her cry out. In and out, he fucked her with his finger, adding another, stretching her, preparing her. Her body responded, climbing towards the peak again. Her inner muscles clenched around his fingers, her clit throbbed, and just as she was about to tumble over the edge, he withdrew his hand.

He entered her again, this time with a swift, hard thrust. She wrapped her legs around him, trying to keep him there, trying to find the rhythm that would send her spiraling. But he held still, denying her the friction she needed. She panted, begged, tried to move against him, but he held her firm, a cruel smile playing on his lips.

"Please," she whimpered, almost in tears from the overwhelming need.

He just chuckled, starting the whole torturous process over again. He played the game for quite some time, stopping his own pleasure each time right before he reached the end.

If he had to suffer, why couldn't she?

"Yes. I think that will be how we control you. I will reward you with your choice of depravity, and not listening will take all of this away. Do you understand?" His fingers were already deep inside her, working in slow, insistent circles against her slick heat, coaxing her closer to the edge with every move.

She was panting desperately, her hips grinding down against his hand, clutching at his wrist for any leverage. "Yes. Anything. Please," she whimpered, her voice hoarse from need.

He grinned and withdrew his hand, leaving her empty for a heartbeat before he dropped to his knees between her spread thighs. He pressed his mouth against her soft folds without hesitation, tongue lashing greedily over her swollen mound while two fingers slid back inside her, curling upward to stroke the spot that made her eyes roll back. She clung to his hair as he devoured her, moaning louder until she was shaking. Just as she tipped over into orgasm, he rode out the spasms with relentless focus, drinking in everything she gave him.

When the tremors slowed, he stood and stroked his cock a few times before lining it up with her soaking entrance. He pushed in with a single thrust; she gasped at the stretch as he filled her. He fucked her hard, one hand braced on the bedframe while the other gripped her hip tight enough to bruise. Their bodies slammed together, both of them lost in the sensations. He could feel her walls flutter around him, his cock dragging in and out until she started coming again and clenched so hard he groaned.

He didn't last much longer after that. When he felt his climax peak, he pulled out just in time to paint streaks of hot cum across her belly and thighs. For a moment, they were both silent except for their breath: hers ragged with aftershocks; his coming down from a growl to a satisfied sigh.

He kissed her once more between the legs before standing straight and smirking down at her limp form. "Remember what happens when you listen," he purred, tracing a line of cum down toward where it dripped from between her legs.

Water splashed over his fingers as he poured from the pitcher, rivulets carrying away the evidence of their encounter. He buttoned his shirt with practiced efficiency, tucking the tails into his trousers. His eyes caught hers in the mirror.

"Oh, Yes, Pet. I will be so good, but I'll expect more rewards like that," she purred.

"Dinner in ten minutes. Be ready," he said, voice low but firm. One eyebrow arched in warning.

"Mmm," she hummed, stretching languidly across the rumpled sheets. Her legs trembled as she finally stood, catching herself against the bedpost when her knees threatened to buckle. A satisfied smile played across her lips as she dabbed a damp cloth between her thighs.

He could see he would need to eat heartily to keep up the energy to deal with her.

For a moment, he breathed. His muscles hummed with exertion and adrenaline, his mind already shifting from flesh to duty. Lydia stretched across the sheets like sin and invitation, but Will knew better than to linger.

Lysa expected them for dinner and he was not willing to risk her ire.

Gorek was already seated when they reached the dining room, his broad shoulders making the old chair beneath him look like a toy. Lysa stood beside him, ladle poised above earthen bowls whose glaze had long since faded from decades of use.

Before Will could make introductions, Lydia's voice cut through the savory aroma of herbs and slow-cooked meat. "The smell of that stew is absolutely divine," she said.

Will noted that her smile did not seem to reach her eyes. It was the practiced politeness of someone in politics. She learned more from the Chancellor than he thought.

"Lydia," Will said, steady but formal, "I'd like you to meet Lysa and Gorek."

Their lined faces betrayed no emotion.

Gorek rose slowly. His shadow stretched with him, swallowing candlelight and casting Lydia in darkness. She instinctively retreated a step and bumped Will's chest. When Gorek finally extended his massive hand, Lydia placed hers inside it with visible hesitation.

Dinner was civil. Barely.

Lysa watched Lydia the way a wolf watches something that might be wounded... or dangerous. Gorek spoke little, with short, noncommittal replies. Lysa refilled his bowl twice, and Gorek's once. Lydia's remained empty until she lifted it herself.

Lydia eventually pushed back her chair with a graceful little yawn. "If you'll excuse me, I think the day has caught up with me."

She departed with murmured thanks and the faint click of her heels vanishing down the hall.

The room exhaled.

Gorek let his shoulders drop. The hard line of his mouth eased. Something softer flickered in his eyes.

Will realized the tension in his own spine only when it finally released.

"Like old times, eh?" Gorek rumbled. His thick Talvian accent softened the words as his weathered hand briefly closed around Will's wrist, grounding him.

In the warm glow from the hearth, Will settled into his chair, watching the ritual unfold. Gorek's massive hands, hands that had snapped bones in the Resistance's darkest operations, now cradled each dish in the washbasin with unexpected gentleness. Lysa received each one, her towel whisking away droplets as their fingers brushed in a dance perfected over decades.

Will's lips curled upward, remembering how he'd watched this same ceremony as a wide-eyed child.

When the last bowl was stowed, they turned to him.

"The heart finds its way eventually," Lysa murmured, her eyes crinkling at the corners.

"What plans chu have?" Gorek asked.

Will filled him in on his plan to leave the city. He was going to get Lydia to safety, then explore the land. He had always wanted to meet the oldest brother of his best friends, Zane and Corben, the twins who had become like brothers when they set sail over the summers, in his work with Gorek and the Resistance. They had each opened taverns, one in the West Woods and the other in Sarhan.

He searched their faces as he finished outlining his plan. Lysa looked pleased. Proud, even. Gorek looked worried.

"Resistance could use chu. Chu have become da best at many thing. But distracted fighters end up dead. Take your time away, then return to us," Gorek said. "I know we had words, but I missed chu and I hope you'll not stay away so long."

He enveloped Will in an embrace that threatened to crack ribs, but the warmth felt good.

It felt like being ten again.

And it hurt, knowing he would just be leaving them again.

As he walked back to the room, his steps faltered. The warmth of Gorek's embrace lingered on his skin, while Lydia's scent still clung to his clothes. The familiar loyalty of the Resistance that had shaped him, or the unknown terrain of a life with her. The option with her was dangerous and intoxicating.

His hand stalled on the knob, unsure which version of himself would enter that room.

CHAPTER 4 –
WAS THIS A MISTAKE?

The axe missed Will's ear by a thickness of paper and buried itself in the alley's plaster with a noise like a wet tooth yanked from gum. He didn't stop to admire the craftsmanship or to ponder the metaphysics of why orc bandits were chasing them with axes, let alone throwing them. He ran, considering picking Lydia up, as her smaller strides were holding him back considerably. They would have been beyond this threat three turns ago if he had.

Lydia's laughter… sharp, delighted, with a hint of psychosis, peeled behind him, pushing him forward. He considered the logistics of grabbing her.

"Left!" She shouted, already catching up to him in his consideration. Her boots slid on the mosaic of ancient piss and discarded food. She glanced back with the mad glee of a woman who had never once in her life regretted an impulsive act.

Will veered left, nearly colliding with a fruit vendor whose entire inventory was displayed on a large wooden cart. The vendor saw Lydia first, and her face went pale as curdled cream. Her hands went up, not slowing her steps much. She grinned wickedly and reached out with her fingers, which were twitching and smoldering.

The vendor's eyes widened. "Don't…"

Too late. Lydia's hand brushed the wooden plank, and flames spat up the length of it, turning the fruit into a bonfire. The vendor screamed… more with insult than injury… and clutched at her smoldering kerchief.

The burning cart blocked access to the alley.

"Let's see them catch us now," Lydia said over her shoulder, her voice smug. She barreled ahead, her hair a red comet in the greasy dusk.

Will looked back, his adrenaline hot in his throat. The orcs, or half-orcs (honestly, Will couldn't tell at a sprint), were only a dozen paces behind, their footsteps pounding the cobbles in a cadence of murderous intent. He risked a glance: three, maybe four of them, all in mismatched armor, tusks out for blood. They shouted something in orcish. The words were lost in the street's echo.

Will had time to regret exactly two things: the first, letting Lydia talk him into this job; the second, not appropriately planning their getaway. Instead, he had a bag of purloined gold… far heavier than Lydia had promised… and their path through the city of Gosual, the old forest city north of the East Draco Mountains, was fraught with hazards. It was also home to the twins' older brother, Gareth.

Lydia caught up to him at a narrow break in the alley. They turned the corner and dipped into a gated building, then locked the door behind them.

"I hope you're planning to compensate her," Will muttered.

Lydia shot him a sideways glance. "Out of my cut or yours?"

"Yours," he said, deadpan.

Climbing stairs and walking down the winding halls, he peeked out of a window to see the orcs reach the corner. Their roars dulled to a grumble as they realized they had lost their prey. Will's heart ratcheted down to a manageable pace.

Will pressed his ear to the wall, holding his breath. Thud. Thud. A splintering crack. Muffled curses in guttural Orcish. Then silence, followed by the shuffle of heavy boots and the clink of weapons being sheathed. Their pursuers' footfalls grew fainter, punctuated by one final, frustrated kick against the door below.

Lydia pressed her ear to the wall, then grinned. "Easy as pie."

Will exhaled, the tension leaving his spine all at once. "You said they'd be outnumbered. You said there'd be two, not four."

"There were two. The others must've been on lunch break. I don't control their schedule."

He shook his head but couldn't help smiling. "You're impossible." This wasn't the first time the information she provided had been off.

She preened, tossing her fire-red mane over one shoulder. "That's why you keep me around."

She started down the pitch-dark corridor, boots muffled on the ancient stone, and then they headed down several sets of stairs. Will fished a penlight from his coat and flicked it on, the beam slicing through a haze of old dust. The safehouse was nothing more than a series of abandoned wine cellars stacked beneath the city's original walls. It was a perfect hideout for the Resistance, and a decent way to stay off the authorities' radar when your last gig went sideways. It might not be sanctioned work, but they wouldn't know he was using the place.

They wound past empty racks and stacked crates, Lydia guiding them by memory more than sight. On the third turn, he stopped, knelt, and pried open a floor hatch. Cold air and the scent of mold drifted up.

"Ladies first," Will said.

Lydia eyed him, then shrugged. She dropped into the hole, landing with the softest of thuds. He passed the sack of gold down, then followed, closing the hatch behind.

The cellar below was barely high enough to stand. Candles guttered in glass jars along the walls, their flames turning the damp stones into a shifting world of shadow and gold. Lydia deposited the bag on a crate and flopped onto a musty pallet. Will watched her, then performed a slow walk around the perimeter, checking for breaches. Old habits never unlearned.

She picked up a coin and flicked it at him. "Sit. You're making me nervous."

He caught the coin and rolled it over his knuckles. Gold, honest currency. Enough here to settle down or at least pay off a lot of angry vendors.

"Did you mean what you said? About giving it to the Resistance?" he asked. His old employers had been sending messages for months, but he ignored them, dropping bags of coin off at known safe houses and offices as was possible.

She lounged, all coiled satisfaction. "I meant what I said about getting paid. If they want to buy my loyalty, they can do it the old-fashioned way."

He shot her a look.

She relented, just a little. "All right. They get most. We keep enough to eat like kings for a week. Or to fix your wardrobe."

He let that slide. The job wasn't supposed to be a haul. It was supposed to give a message to the orc syndicates that they weren't as untouchable as they thought, and that the Resistance had teeth. Lydia had improved the plan, as usual, by doubling the risk and the payout.

He might not be officially working for the Resistance, but his choice of targets was graded on how much benefit it would give to others, as well as himself. He liked to think of them as vigilantes of sorts, working on their own for the greater good. Lydia just wanted the most fun.

"You're not worried about the Guild?" he asked. "That's twice in as many weeks we've clipped their purse. One of these days, they will catch on, even if they are Orcs."

She smiled, teeth white and sharp. "I'm counting on it. Let them come. They have nothing on us."

He admired her confidence, even if it bordered on suicidal. He wondered, sometimes, how much of it was shown and how much was genuine. He'd never been able to tell.

Travel with Lydia was a vector for trouble, not distance. In Media, she had grown accustomed to a high-party girl lifestyle. The lifestyle she enjoyed came at a high price, but she was fun… or at least she was when they met over a year ago. When the time dawned on him… it sank in what a rollercoaster of life he had been on since that day. He lost track of time.

That first month alone… By the time they reached Sarhan, Will had lost track of how many towns they'd been run out of, or how many times he'd watched Lydia charm their way out of mortal peril by sheer force of personality and, when that failed, by setting things on fire.

Since then, they had burned the bridges with most of the ships captains, though only one had been burned literally. As a result, they had to resort to traveling to Aloria with the merchant caravans, until, inevitably, they stole something or she slept with the wrong person. Every town was like the last.

They had spent the last few months making random attacks on the Orc syndicate, Media guards, Slavers of Fellspire Citadel, and other bandits. At least he had felt that their fun had also benefited someone who needed it. At night, she'd lie out the coins on the table and make patterns to see the way the candlelight flickered off the stamped faces, as she had that night.

She lounged on the pallet, sifting the coins into a spiral on the splintered floor. "I love the shine that comes from the coins spilled out," she declared to him one night.

"Some of the money should be used to help people. We have more than enough." He sipped his wine, admiring the flavor. "We don't need to keep this up. We should use this money to get a life."

She flopped on the bed, arms out, letting the coins scatter. "You're no fun lately, Pet." He hated the nickname she coined for him, but if he said anything, she just used it even more.

He raised an eyebrow. "We set fire to a watchtower this morning. The watchtower is used to protect the city. Now, how will the people be able to watch for raiders?"

She held up a finger. "You know what your problem is?" Lydia said, not waiting for him to answer. "You keep thinking you can clear your ledger with good deeds."

Will looked at her, at the sharpness in her face, the hunger that never quite went away. "What does that mean?"

She smiled, a little sad. "It means you should stop pretending you're the good guy and just enjoy life."

Her words bit, too close to the truth.

He watched her, noting how her hair caught the flicker, and how she could shift from lethal to childlike in a single glance. It used to thrill him. Now it just made him tired.

They sat in silence, listening to the rumble of the city above. He finally sat beside her on the pallet, smelling the smoke and expensive shampoo of her hair. For a while, they just existed, neither speaking.

"Maybe we should take a break from this stuff for a while. There is excitement, but... I feel like I need more," he said, eyeing her earnestly.

She leaned in and moved closer, looking at him as if she were trying to read his soul. That sat for a moment.

She could be so present and caring at times.

Finally, Lydia said, "We'll get this figured out. We could leave, you know. Find somewhere quiet. Start over."

He considered it. When he was young, he thought of opening the bakery his father had dreamed of and thought about the possibility of waking up somewhere that wasn't the slums of Talvi in Media, or backwoods city like Gosual, or any of the other towns choking themselves to death on their own secrets. That dream wasn't what he really wanted, but he knew he needed something more than this.

But then he thought about the Resistance, about the work that still needed to be done. He hated that there were children in Media who might be dealing with the loss of their family, as he had.

Lydia, for better or worse, was fun and kept him entertained, but he was starting to think he wanted... no... needed more.

"I don't know what I want to do," he confessed. "We left Media over a year ago, and this... this life is getting stale." He winced as he spoke, knowing she would be upset.

"So, I'm stale," she pouted.

"You aren't stale. This..." he motioned around them. "This is getting stale. This is the life I thought I wanted, but now that I have it... It isn't measuring up." No need to hide the truth from her. She wasn't going to like it, but it needed to be said.

He closed his eyes as the room went silent for a moment so that he could prepare for her reaction.

He waited for her to cry or get emotional, but... instead... she did what he hadn't expected. She prowled over to him with a gleam in her eye, threw herself onto his lap, and pressed her lips to his.

He stiffened. Mind you, Lydia was a certified sex fiend, but he had expected her to fall apart. He had just commented that he was not happy with the relationship, and she thought sex would improve things. It made no sense.

She noticed he didn't reciprocate and stopped.

"We could bring someone up. Threesomes are always so much fun," she said, looking him in the eye. "That girl from the common room is dying for it. Her tits are beautiful, and I saw her wink at you. I bet she would be pretty tasty, too. I saw her eating some of that fruit that I like."

He shook his head and stood up, extricating her from his lap. She didn't get it, and it is possible she never would.

"I never thought I would ever hear myself say that I am not interested in sex with two women... I'm not in the mood. I'm fine if you want to enjoy her yourself."

"Suit yourself. I'm going to talk to her." She walked toward the door, seemingly already bored. Maybe she would find his replacement while he was out. One could only hope.

Her sex addiction was a point of contention. She would find another woman, since he refused to share with another guy. Their negotiation was that she could have all the women she wanted, but she mistakenly thought he wanted them also and usually brought them back to share with him. Having extra sex constantly sounded like a dream come true... at first, but meaningless sex was losing its pull. She would bring them to the room, they would begin having sex in front of him, then Lydia would do something to drag him into things. It was just a matter of time till it happened again.

After he cleaned up the coins and stored them away, Will stretched out on the bed and closed his eyes. He was exhausted, but sleep had lately been a traitor.

It seemed like only a few minutes later that he heard two female voices in the corridor. The conversation was mostly laughter, punctuated by the clink of glass, then the sound of the door opening to their suite.

He looked up to see Lydia smiling against the brunette's lips, as she led her by the hip to the bed where Will was sitting. The woman's smile broadened when she turned and raked her eyes over his lounging form.

"Lydia. I thought we talked about this," he said, but his voice lacked conviction. His eyes were already drawn to the brunette's curves, her heavy breasts, and the tattoo that accentuated her waist.

"Will. Meet Nala. She says she has never tried with three before. She was excited at the thought," Lydia said proudly. He shook his head but made no other movement.

Lydia ignored his half-hearted protest, her fingers deftly unbuttoning his shirt. She pushed it off his shoulders, her nails grazing his skin, leaving goosebumps in their wake. The brunette, meanwhile, went straight for his belt, unbuckling it quickly before unbuttoning the leathers. Will lifted his hips slightly, allowing her to tug off his pants in one smooth motion. His cock sprang free, already half-hard... just because his head wasn't into it didn't mean his body wasn't.

The brunette didn't waste any time and seemed to forget that Lydia was in the room for a moment. She wrapped her hand around his shaft, her thumb circling the sensitive tip. Moving to a half-seated position leaning against the pillows, Will groaned, his head falling back against the headboard, his arms splayed over the headboard, opening himself to their attention.

On all fours, the brunette leaned down, her tongue flicking out to lick the bead of pre-cum from his slit. She looked up at him, their eyes meeting as she took him into her mouth. He groaned again, louder this time, as she began to bob her head, her lips creating a tight seal around his cock as Lydia stood to the side, stripped, and surveyed the scene. Lydia lay down between the woman's legs, then pulled her to sit on her face.

Moments later, he saw Lydia motion for the brunette to sit up, though her mouth continued working, then she moved up to get an up-close view of the ministrations being performed on him. She positioned herself behind the brunette. Leaning in, she gently brushed the woman's hair to one side, exposing the nape of her neck. Lydia softly kissed the newly exposed skin. Her hands, tentative at first, began to explore the brunette's body, tracing the curve of her waist and the flare of her hips as she continued her attentions to him. Watching her enjoy the woman's body was quite a turn on, and his erection grew of its own accord.

Will followed Lydia's fingertips with his eyes as they lightly grazed the woman's thigh, resulting in a shiver that made her pause in her efforts to him. When Lydia entered her folds, she stopped mid-suck and replaced her sweet lips with her hand. Lydia's hands must have found the right spots, as the brunette responded with a soft moan, pressing back against Lydia's touch and raising to show him her hard nipples.

He lay back, knowing that Lydia would manage to ensure this was a long night. He just needed to bask in the ride. He couldn't resist cupping the brunette's ample breasts himself and working her pebbled nipples. They were like ripe melons... Lydia's favorite, though he didn't mind them either. Between the two of them, they coaxed a climax out of her.

With his erection at full length, Lydia gently guided the brunette's head away so that she could position herself above him as he lay back on the bed, while the woman teased Lydia's breasts with fingers and tongue. Lydia's body was flushed with arousal, her breath coming in short gasps as she straddled his hips. She reached down, her fingers wrapping around his shaft. She guided him to her entrance; his tip could feel her slick wetness. He could feel her body tense in anticipation as she slowly lowered herself onto him. She rode him up and down, undulating to a rhythm only she could hear; the silence of the room was punctuated with her moans and gasps.

Although she had climaxed several times, Lydia would not let him finish. This had become the norm, though. He knew what to expect. As soon as she sensed his climax coming, she would stop... to prolong her pleasure. He could have forced the issue, but that wasn't his way. She had flipped his initial punishment on him, and he wasn't a fan.

As it was, he felt like he was only a tool for her, with him moving where she wanted and performing as requested. It took the fun out of it for him. He still participated and enjoyed it, but it was more about the process than the passion.

His heart just wasn't in it.

At some point, she allowed him to climax, and he fell dead asleep, realizing that he needed something more. He had only really opened up to two other women before this. He doubted if he would ever be able to open up to another woman again. Angel had been his youth, a love of a high school boy. Only a few years later, he had met Felicity. He had really thought she was the one. He had picked out a ring and was about to propose when she had disappeared.

Maybe this thing with Lydia was as good as he would ever have, but he hoped not. He would never know if he were still with her, though maybe he didn't deserve more.

Will had been able to leave the room before either woman had awoken. He wandered the old town, bought a paper cone of sugared nuts, and watched the local kids run scams on the tourists. He thought about Lydia, about the magnetism that pulled him back to her every time, no matter how many times he tried to leave her orbit. He thought about how, for all her wildness, Lydia never really seemed lost. She always knew exactly what she wanted, even if it changed by the hour.

He, on the other hand, didn't know where he wanted to go. When he was young, his focus was only on being the best Resistance operative he could be, to stop the city that killed his family. Once he had excelled at that, it began to feel like he could never overcome the obstacle, so why fight and kill at the direction of a group that might not be any better than the city?

He spent the next few hours soul-searching to try to find a direction that would bring him peace, but after all that time, he still didn't feel as though he knew what his next steps should be.

When he returned to the inn, the room was empty, except for a folded note propped on the bed. Lydia had gone to the docks. She suggested he join her and signed the note with a lipstick kiss.

He ignored it.

Instead, he stretched out on the mattress, boots still on, and tried to nap. The sun was down when he heard the tap-tap at the door.

He didn't answer. The door opened anyway, and he glanced over, expecting to see the little pixie walking in.

A bald man entered with a fake smile that didn't quite reach his eyes. Will sat up, his hand on his knife, his reflexes primed for trouble.

"Evening," the man said, closing the door behind him.

Will nodded, keeping his hands visible. "Lost?"

The man grinned, showing gold teeth. "Not anymore. Got a package for you."

He tossed a small envelope onto the bed, then walked out the door, closing it behind him. Will caught it, felt the ridges under the paper. There was a double seal, Resistance style. He didn't open it until the man was gone.

In some ways, he was a bit surprised they had found him here; in other ways, he wasn't. He had given that life up when he left with Lydia, as she had convinced him to focus on fun instead of responsibility. It looked like that life would never leave him for good.

Inside, there was a sliver of a card, with nothing but a series of dots and dashes punched along one edge.

Will laughed. Old school. Very old school. He could only think of a few operatives he worked with who would still use that system.

He pulled out his knife and pried the card apart along the seam. Sure enough, inside was a secondary strip, this one inked with a single word in block capitals: TONIGHT.

He ran his thumb over the dots, letting the muscle memory take over. The rhythm came back to him, a nervous tic he thought he'd outgrown. He tapped the code on his knee, translating as he went.

Rendezvous at the clock tower,
sundown. Alone. No followers. See you soon
Hawk.

He almost choked. He hadn't heard his Resistance code name for a while. He missed it, as it had been a part of him for so long.

He stared at the card, his pulse thumping at the opportunity to return to his old life. The message was clear enough. What wasn't clear was why now, or who'd sent it. Gorek hated those bumps; he never used them. His fingers were too big. He and Angel had spent months learning to read them. She had always liked how simple it was. The messages could be kept in plain sight and never found.

He thought about leaving it alone. He thought about burning the message, packing his bag, and vanishing before sundown. He even stood up, looked out the window, and calculated how long it would take to reach the edge of town on foot. He had been asking for something different, and it had shown up.

Why did he want Lydia to join him? Wasn't he thinking he was going to leave?

But old habits won. They always did. He wasn't sure if this was a real meeting. It would be beneficial to have some backup, after all.

He pocketed the card, then went to find Lydia.

He found her on the docks, as advertised, smoking a contraband clove and watching the sunset.

She grinned when she saw him. "Miss me?"

He ignored the question. "We have to go."

She arched an eyebrow. "Oh? Date night?"

"Not exactly."

She flicked the roll into the water, then fell into step beside him, not even asking where they were headed.

As they walked, Will ran a thumb over the edge of the card, feeling the raised bumps. Lydia noticed.

"What's got you so wound up?" she said, voice low.

"Nothing," he said, too quickly.

She smiled, catlike. "If you're lying to me, at least make it interesting."

He didn't answer. He just kept walking, Lydia's short legs barely keeping up at his side, the clock tower already visible against the bruise-purple sky.

Whatever waited for them at the top, Will told himself he was ready.

He almost believed it. They had arrived early so that he could surveil the area. Checking. It didn't seem anything was out of place.

The clock tower rose above the rooftops like a snapped bone, jagged and impossible to ignore. Will counted the windows as they approached, everyone a potential kill zone. The last of the sun was a smear of orange, staining the broken glass. Lydia walked beside him, silent for once, her hair bright as a warning flare.

He kicked himself. He had lost so many of his cautious ways of dealing with her.

The street was empty, but shadows pooled in every doorway, every broken cart and sagging archway. He saw nothing, which meant nothing; the Resistance wasn't in the habit of making things easy.

At the tower's base, the old iron door was unlatched. Lydia ran a finger over the rusted hinge that creaked loudly as she pushed it and raised an eyebrow. "Subtle," she said.

He rolled his eyebrows at her. How could she not know at this point that they were supposed to squeeze through without opening the gate, not to make noise?

The smell inside was old wood and ancient dust. The staircase was spiral, half-collapsed in places, the stone steps mottled with generations of pigeon shit and rainwater. He gestured for Lydia to follow, then paused, reconsidered. There was no chance for stealth if he brought her up with him.

"Wait here," he said, voice low.

She pouted. "What if someone tries to attack me?"

He knew better. She wasn't as helpless as she liked to act. He hadn't known her to look someone in the eyes when she killed, but he knew her fires had taken several people out. "You know how to take care of yourself. If you have issues... yell."

She laughed and leaned against the wall, posing as if she were waiting for a lover rather than a clandestine meeting. Will headed up the stairs, with his senses on high alert.

Every step echoed up and down the shaft. He kept his body close to the inner wall, minimizing his silhouette. At the third landing, he heard the faint click of a boot on stone, timed precisely to the tick of the clockworks overhead.

He didn't hesitate. He kept moving, rounding the curve, hand ready at his hip for his knife.

At the top, the bell chamber was just as he remembered: a cavern of shadow and moonlight, with a forest of wooden supports, and a few brave pigeons.

The shadow moved slightly into the light, and his breath caught. Even with the slightly longer hair, he would know the curve of that neck and wicked gleam in her eye anywhere.

Angel waited in the far corner, leaning against a strut. The scar on her jaw looked fresher in the cold light. Her curves were just as deadly as he remembered. He looked around, but they were alone.

She watched him cross the room, not moving, not speaking.

He stopped just out of arm's reach. They stood there, two statues, the silence between them a wall.

"Will," she said, finally. He wasn't sure how to take her tone.

"Angel," he replied. He tried to hide his excitement at seeing her again.

She shook her head, almost smiled. "You're late."

"Liar," he said. "You know I'm right on time."

Her eyes flicked past him to the stairs. "Still with the Redhead, I see. I thought I warned you about her?"

He shrugged. "She's impossible to leave behind."

Angel's gaze softened, then sharpened again. "She's a liability."

"So am I," he said.

They stood in silence, letting the truth of it settle. Angel was right. He probably should have left her behind. Hell. He probably should never have accepted the job in the first place.

Angel straightened and crossed her arms over her chest. "You look like hell."

"You've seen me look worse," he toyed with a crooked grin.

She tilted her head, acknowledging the point. "Why haven't you responded to the Resistance messages?"

He considered lying, decided not to bother. "I was trying to find a different life."

"Why did you answer this one then?"

"Maybe I didn't like the life I found," he said with a level of honesty he hadn't expected to admit to. Maybe it was their history. Angel was his first romantic partner and the first one he killed for. At a time when he felt the need to return to his old life, honesty felt appropriate.

She looked at him for a long time, as if weighing what that meant. Finally, she said, "You know why you're here?"

"Not a clue. When I saw the code, I had a feeling it was you."

She smiled, but it didn't reach her eyes. "You're the best we've got. Or you were. Are you still?" He hated how good she was at hiding her feelings. He couldn't read her. Never could.

He didn't answer.

A long moment passed. The only sounds were the tick of the clock and the wind through the gaps in the masonry.

Angel uncrossed her arms, walked to the center of the chamber, and beckoned him closer. He followed, cautious.

"We need you to steal something," she said. They were so close that the smell of her enveloped him. She had a natural musk to her that drew him in. He had to hold back his desire to touch her.

"Sounds like a classic heist. There are better thieves out there than me. Not many... but..." he offered, making sure the dimple that he knew she loved so much showed.

She ignored the sarcasm. "It's a book, and we have already lost three teams retrieving it. It's old, dangerous, and locked up in the vault... within the Order of Tamris."

He arched an eyebrow. "The Order's vault? That's a suicide mission. So, you need someone who can get into the inner sanctum past an army of trained assassins, break into a vault that is protected technically, magically, and physically, and then get an item out while staying alive... knowing that the Order is one of the most vindictive groups on the planet. They have been known to wipe out entire villages to get to one person."

She nodded.

He whistled. "You do like making things complicated."

Angel glanced at the stairs again. "Does that mean you won't do it?"

"I didn't say that."

"Does she know what you are?"

He grinned. "She knows I'm with the Resistance, but she thinks I'm a basic thief."

"And if she learns otherwise?"

"She won't, and if anything, that might turn her on more." He had hoped that comment would elicit some reaction from her. As he still couldn't read anything, maybe she wasn't interested in him. Perhaps she really was that desperate that she had to come to him.

Angel looked unconvinced. "The book is cursed... or protected... or both. We've lost three teams already."

Will felt a chill crawl up his back. "And you want me to try next? What would it matter if I die? No one left to miss me."

"I want you to do what you do best," Angel said, with a softening in her tone. "Survive. You were my top pick from the beginning. I know you can do it."

He studied her, trying to read between the lines. She looked tired, brittle, like the years had worn her down to a single point of willpower. He felt sorry for her and hated himself for it.

"You could just walk away," Angel said, voice almost gentle. "And I wouldn't blame you. It is likely a suicide mission. I'm trying to bring together the best I can to help you."

"I've tried," he said, not sure if she was referring to the pixie or the job. Either way... it was the same answer. "Never sticks."

She nodded, as if she'd expected that.

The sound of a footstep on the stairs made them turn. Lydia stood at the top of the stairs, attempting to peek in.

Angel's eyes narrowed and whispered. "You trust her?"

Will thought about it and whispered back. "No, but I know her, and she is fearless. Exactly what we need in a suicide mission."

Angel gave a small, tight smile. "That's not saying much."

He shrugged. "It's all I've got."

She sighed and rubbed the scar on her jaw. "Bring her in then. She needs to hear this, too."

He motioned for Lydia to walk closer, then watched her make her way up to him, curving into him, placing his arms around her, as she stood in front of him.

She sized up Angel in an instant, eyes taking in every detail. Angel stood as typical, with her weapon hidden in her jacket, the old tattoo peeking from her wrist. Lydia's smile held, but her pupils shrank, not out of fear, but of challenge.

Angel provided a basic explanation: the Resistance needed someone to break into a vault and steal something of value that was difficult. Angel explained the high-level plan, with maps, codes, the time, and the exact locations of places. She avoided some of the more dangerous aspects. She already had others identified to help. Will listened, absorbing every detail, every possible trap. Lydia looked bored until the word "vault" came up, then her eyes lit with a new kind of hunger. He had worked with Angel long enough to know she usually provided much more detail. He assumed that the lack of information was due to Lydia. Angel didn't trust her, and for good reason.

When Angel finished, silence settled over the bell chamber. She watched him, waiting for questions.

"It tracks," Will said after a beat. "I'm assuming you will have more details when I get there."

Then he turned to Lydia. "This will be fun." It was all she needed at the moment.

Lydia smirked, predatory and pleased. "So, what do we get out of this?"

Angel didn't react. "This is the mission…"

Will cut across her with nothing but a look and a slow shake of his head.

"You will get your share of coin," Will said evenly. He held Angel's gaze, hoping she recognized that he was saying exactly what Lydia needed to hear and nothing more.

Lydia considered him. "You in?"

He looked at Angel. Then at Lydia. Then at the night outside the broken window, where the sky was dark and full of teeth.

He nodded.

Angel smiled, and this time it reached her eyes. "Then the others will meet you in the safe house inside the Citadel. Do you still remember the route?"

"It's been a while, but I remember," Will confirmed.

The plan was set. The game was on.

And for the first time in years, Will felt alive.

CHAPTER 5 –
PLANNING THE IMPOSSIBLE

Will tracked each robed figure of the Order of Tamris guards, counting off the seconds between their rotation points. The courtyard was never truly still. Torches crackled against the rain-dark stone. Orders were barked. Boots clicked with ritual precision. The tedium was occasionally broken by the barked orders of an officer or the flicker of a torch illuminating the rain-slick flagstones.

Four months of hard travel had finally brought them here on foot. They watched from a third-story window across a narrow, refuse-choked street. The Citadel of Eternal Vigil glowed under torchlight, guarded by men and women in featureless white robes. Faces hidden. Movements identical. No hesitation. No wasted motion.

The guards were known as Disciples, though they performed the same duty. They were all dressed in white, their hoods drawn and faces obscured. Each was a precise cog in the city's new regime of magical control.

The waning moon over the city of Sanctus was a half-blind eye, casting a smear across the broken spires of the East City, as the sun prepared its return. From the third-story window of the large housing complex, which also included an inn that housed many of the Votaries or foot soldiers of the Order, the building's skeletal walls provided a nearly perfect vantage point.

At the far wall of the room, Lydia perched on a rusted heating pipe with her legs crossed. She wore the full regalia of a junior priestess, stolen earlier from the corpse cooling at her feet. Her hands, deft and practiced, fussed with the headpiece, adjusting the silver-embroidered headpiece with unnecessary flair. She made the macabre look theatrical.

Will lowered the spyglass, rubbing the ache from his brow. "They're early."

Lydia didn't bother looking over. She pinned the skirt shorter so it wouldn't drag. "Maybe word got out about their two missing Disciples. I think I got the placement right, so it looks like they were fucking and then attacked."

Will glanced down at the bodies. Naked, arranged, blood pooling in a precise line across the tile. Indeed, Lydia's placement made it appear as though they were caught in the act and killed, disturbingly effective. Blood had pooled and begun to run. He made a note to ensure he did not step in it. He turned back to the window, not out of squeamishness but out of protocol. Staring at your own work was unprofessional.

"You going sentimental, Pet?" Lydia asked lightly.

He ignored the nickname he had grown to hate.

The deaths hadn't been satisfying. Necessary, yes. Clean, efficient, purposeful. If these Tomes were as valuable as Angel said they were... their deaths would help thousands. Will did not enjoy killing. He was good at it. And in a world choking itself on corruption, skill mattered more than intent.

"I'm worried that this will raise flags," he said. "We do not want patrols sweeping alleys before we reach the safehouse."

Lydia snorted. "If they do, we improvise. That's the fun part, right?"

Will did not answer. Improvisation was the fastest route to a grave.

Lydia completed her task and moved to his side, the priestess's robes swirling as she crossed the room. The pinning was barely noticeable. "How's the timing looking?" she asked, running a thumb along the hem of her sleeve.

Will checked his battered notebook, the cover patched with tape and filth. He'd diagrammed the courtyard: gate, columns, torch positions, each guard with a penciled-in sweep line showing their field of vision.

"Thirty-six seconds per sweep. Four seconds blind spot at the southeast pillar. But the captain is random. Like yesterday. If we need to get in at this time of morning, it will be a challenge to get through these gates. Morning seems to be our best chance."

She tugged her headpiece lower, eyes glinting beneath the fringe. "They'll never expect a woman of the cloth."

"That's if they believe you are one. Just wearing the robes isn't enough. They will not if you swagger like that or drink from the bottle. You need to look pious, not like you intend to rob the vault and sleep with the Votaries."

He flipped the notebook shut, then packed his gear with quiet ritual. Lockpicks. Crushed glass packet. Fuse strip. Filed-off mag pistol. Each item was placed with practiced calm.

He strapped the Order-issued holster to his thigh. He preferred knives, but no one walked armed near the Citadel unless they were ordained. The Order of Tamris believed discipline was the act of faith, and violence was the doctrine.

As such, there were strict rules in the city surrounding their Citadel. No weapons for anyone other than Disciples,

Votaries, and Priestesses. He wasn't about to be left weaponless, surrounded by some of the best assassins in the world.

Even if he didn't appreciate their devotion to their God, he could appreciate their lifelong dedication to the art of killing. If he hadn't been in Media and found the Resistance, he could have seen the appeal to the Order.

Dressed as they were, they could go down to the Order-heavy tavern of the inn, then attempt to go through the gates of the Citadel past the guards. He wasn't as confident in not being stopped. He was taller than average, but he could carry himself like the killing machines the Disciples were. He could blend in.

It was Lydia he doubted. Her height was shorter than the average priestess, and the idea that she could ever pass for a pious Disciple, even in a crowd, was almost absurd after seeing her hips sway in her robes.

The rest of the team should meet them at the safehouse within an hour. Having a Resistance base underneath the Citadel within the walls was genius, but risky. If they could get in without being seen, it was a good thing there were safer ways to get to the safehouse within the walls.

He ran a final check: gloves on, faces shadowed, nothing left behind but the footprints in the dust. Will motioned for Lydia to go through the window, where the decayed ledge promised a two-meter drop to the next rooftop. Lydia went first, her small frame vaulting over with feline grace. Her landing was silent. Will followed, heavier but no less practiced, his knees bending to absorb the impact.

They moved in tandem, keeping low along the building's spine. In the air, the Temple's bell tolled, echoing through the empty streets. The sound drew every guard's head to the main gate.

Just as Will planned.

Six seconds of distraction, enough time for them to get past without being seen.

They slid down a rusted drainpipe, their boots scraping the stone. At street level, the city reeked of mildew and the lingering scent of last year's fires. Will had memorized the route to the entrance: two turns, a sharp left behind the shuttered herbalist, then down a narrow alley.

He caught sight of the stables ahead. Two large stable hands worked nearby, each performing their tasks with watchful eyes. The larger of the two turned to him as he approached.

"Can I help you with something, Votary?" the man asked, his deep bass attempting to sound subservient, but with an underlying menace.

He stopped brushing the horse and moved toward the tools hanging on the wall. It seemed his disguise looked authentic, as he was addressed as a dedicated follower.

"We seek truth in Vigil," Will responded with the coded message, holding his hands out to show he was not a threat.

"Truth waits for the True Command," the guard responded warily.

"The Command speaks only in the Shadow," Will gave the final response expected.

Recognition loosened the man's stance. He gave a short, almost imperceptible nod to the other stable hand, who had stopped baling hay from a distance. He returned to brushing the horse. "Angel said you'd be expected and would know the way."

Leaving the men to their work, Will led Lydia into the stable, then found the stall third from the end. He pressed three of the ten dots painted on the side of the crate sitting in the corner. He smiled when he heard the click and thud of the lock releasing. Sliding the crate aside, the entrance to the service tunnel was revealed.

They ducked inside, following the steps down into the darkness. He heard Lydia curse under her breath as she tripped in the dark, then a small ball of fire formed in her palm.

"It wouldn't kill them to put a light source down here," she complained.

"Yes. They should have lit the clandestine entrance to tunnels that shouldn't exist, connecting directly to the Order's servant tunnels. Should we put up signs, too?" Will whispered, his sarcasm carrying through the tunnels.

As soon as he finished speaking, he realized the small light in his hand was woefully inadequate. She might have a point. He needed to maneuver for the first trap and would need more light.

With a bit of sweetness in his tone, he asked, "Can you brighten the light a bit over here?" He motioned toward the floor in front of him.

She scoffed but obeyed, giving him a better view of the pattern on the floor. "We can only step on the blue squares until we reach the next turn," he said as he took the next step. Luckily, the squares were just large enough for his oversized feet.

Once they passed that obstacle, Will counted his steps carefully, following the instructions he had memorized. Other than the occasional sigh or squelch of disgust from Lydia, they walked in silence through the one thousand five hundred steps within the honeycomb of intersecting passageways.

After several twists and turns, they neared what looked like a trash-filled alcove. Will's arm shot out, blocking Lydia's path.

"Whatever you do, don't touch anything above your waist. Our entrance is at the end, but it won't be good."

"I didn't want to touch anything anyway." Lydia's nostrils flared as her gaze swept over the filth. Her shoulders rose and fell with a dramatic sigh.

He stayed close as they inched their way into the hallway.

As he expected, her boot caught an uneven stone. She stumbled forward, her arm flailing for balance, allowing her fingers to brush against a splintered crate. A metallic click echoed through the tunnel.

Will lunged, yanking her sideways as something whistled past. Lydia's hand flew to her ear, coming away with a smear of blood where the dart had nicked her.

"You alright?" he murmured.

As she nodded, he checked her for any additional injuries and found her otherwise fine. He raised his eyebrow as he added, "It's booby-trapped, if I wasn't clear before. Darts will shoot out."

Turning, he continued to pick his way through the obstacles, leading the way with only her small flame as a light source.

"What do they use these tunnels for anyway?" Lydia asked, her disdain from the atmosphere of decay and despair too obvious.

"These tunnels move slaves and remove their dead. It raises fewer questions for their holy mission if they don't have the population seeing how many bodies they go through," Will spat quietly, thinking of the innocent people who were brought to train the Disciples.

He saw her wrinkle her nose in the dim flamelight.

"The Resistance spent considerable effort adding to the tunnel system, including a few private entrances and rooms, in the hopes of helping some of their slaves escape. Thankfully, we have mapped most of their tunnels."

"I'm surprised they aren't used more," she stated.

"One or two slaves can go missing, and the Order is disappointed, but not upset. Even with one or two, they may come after them; any more slaves, and we risk being found, much less their retribution for taking from their God. They are very quick to take offense, and any offense is handled with swift and painful justice."

At the very end of the tunnel, on the left side behind a pile of crates, was a narrow entrance to an access tunnel. Will squeezed through, his oversized shoulders barely fitting.

They emerged into a concrete box barely larger than a closet. A bolted steel wall marked what Will knew to be the door to their safehouse. Unless a person inspected closely, they might not even realize it was a door, since there was no handle.

With only Lydia's flame for light, Will knelt and traced the wall until his fingers found the recessed keypad. It flickered awake under his touch, symbols shifting like a code alive. When he selected the first symbol, the order of the symbols changed until he entered all six memorized symbols. At the final symbol, he was gratified to hear the tumblers give way with a click. The steel wall eased open slowly, and they slipped inside. After they passed, he pressed a button on the inside to the right of the doorway, which closed the door behind them.

The safehouse was just as he remembered it from years before... a cement-encased hole in the ground, a cellar dug beneath a tannery under the Citadel. The place reeked of ancient chemical rot, every surface slick with a film of grease and mildew, but it was secure.

It was nothing more than a single large room, a foot taller than him, with three smaller rooms and a basic bathroom with magical piping. Glowing crystals provided the light underground.

The main room was sparse, with only a counter, a sink, a metal table, and four chairs. Two smaller rooms had just enough space for a small cot.

The third room had a darker purpose. The blood-spattered walls and drain gave a clear indication of the room's purpose for interrogations, and the smell of fresh blood showed it had been used recently.

"A torture closet and mildew crystals," Lydia muttered. "I've stayed in broom cupboards with better ambiance."

After clearing the space to ensure they were alone, Will sat at the table watching Lydia's disparaging assessment of the place. He searched the area for hidden switches and bugs. With the threat of the Order and the subpar facilities, this was one of his least favorite safe houses and cities to travel to. Lydia's bougie lifestyle seemed to have rubbed off in more ways than he thought.

"What are you doing?" Lydia asked.

"Looking for the switch that will open the vault and making sure there aren't any listening devices. Angel said there would be dossiers, job information, and weapons here. I don't see anything lying out, so it must be hidden. Help me find the latch." When he finished checking the table, he moved to the counter.

"This place is a dump. How long are we expected to stay in… this?" She turned up her nose and grazed her fingers over the bed frame in one of the rooms before sitting on the mattress.

"I know it's not up to your standards, but this was all the Resistance could spare for a safe house in Sanctus. They typically avoid anything to do with these fanatics, as they are known for violent retribution and all," Will responded as he stood to examine the counter space.

After a few moments, his fingertip landed on a raised surface. He pressed it lightly and felt it move. A click and whoosh sounded on the wall where a latch released, revealing a large, hidden compartment containing weapons, folders, and a sack of coins neatly blending into the wall.

He flipped open the first folder. Ink maps. Guard rotations. Names.

The clock in his head ticked down. Less than an hour until the schedule reset.

The others still needed to make it through the gates.

Lydia yanked off the headpiece and tossed it onto the cot. Her hair, freed, fell across her eyes in a crimson curtain. She looked at him, then at the table, then back.

"You hungry?" she said, deadpan, hiking her skirt up, revealing she wore nothing beneath. With a sly smile, she added, "There is a bed... we have some time to wait. How 'bout a quick one?"

He ignored her, continuing his methodical review of the documents.

She huffed in irritation, walking to the bathroom and shutting the door. She came out shortly and milled around the room, running her hands over his shoulders as she passed him.

Eventually, she flopped onto the bed, stretching luxuriously. "Are you going to make me take care of myself?" she asked in a huff.

"This is my priority. Sorry." He focused on the folders, not caring what she was doing in the room.

Reading the note left for him, he realized the documents were dossiers on each of the fifteen team members Angel had planned to ask. He wondered which ones would be crazy enough to take the job. He knew some; others, he had heard, had reputations of their own. He needed at least a five-person crew, but he hoped for the full eight.

How was he supposed to put a complete plan together when he didn't even know who was going to be helping him?

"You ever think about what you'll do when this is over?" she asked.

He glanced at her, then at the ceiling, which dripped with condensation. "Doesn't pay to plan that far ahead, especially with this job... I need to concentrate."

"Fine," she moved to the bedroom.

Boots scraped on the stone outside the door, then a muffled shout, followed by the clatter of armor. He checked his mag-pistol and the collection of blades secured to him, then pressed his ear to the wall.

He waited for the noise to pass, then nodded to Lydia, who had just begun to reapply the head covering. "I assume this is more of the team. Be prepared... in case."

She sprang from the cot, rolling her shoulders.

A patterned rap sounded at the door, letting him know an ally waited for him on the other side.

He triggered the door cautiously.

His hand dropped to his holster, but he relaxed as Kell slipped through, followed by Dorna. He recognized them from a past job and the dossiers, but he didn't know them well.

Kell was the kind of thief who looked like one, all sharp angles and nervous energy. His hair was shaved on the sides, the top kept in a messy braid threaded with bits of copper wire and, Will now noticed, at least three different lockpicks. His eyes were quick and hungry.

Dorna, in contrast, was a slab of muscle poured into a guard uniform, her hands scarred and blackened from years of chemical burns. She carried a battered duffel that jangled as she set it down, the metallic chime of explosive components instantly recognizable.

Kell flicked his gaze around the room, nodding at Will, then at Lydia. "I'm guessing you're Hawk. Angel sent us."

Will grunted, waving them in. "I've been reading up on your skill sets. Impressive." They smelled like field operatives.

Not recruits. Not theorists. People who'd survived mistakes. The kind he could work with.

Kell grinned, unzipping his jacket to reveal a mesh vest lined with tools. "I get into things. She gets us out." He thumbed at Dorna, who was already unpacking vials and setting them upright on the table with loving precision.

Will watched as Kell withdrew an impossible array of tools, gadgets, and contraptions, some larger than the bag itself, until they were covering the table. The pile grew until it threatened to spill onto the floor.

"That bag of yours," Will finally said, gesturing at the mountain of equipment. "Some kind of magical trick, or are you just really good at packing?"

Kell's grin sharpened. "Magical. Yes. I actually won it in a card game, if you can believe it. The last owner said it was a one-off, made just for them by a high priest of Lumara."

He held out the empty leather bag with a stage magician's flourish, then reached inside and pulled out, impossibly, a full-sized crowbar, then a second, then a steel rod that looked long enough to bar a castle gate. "It doesn't work on living things, though. Tried it once," he added, glancing at Dorna. "Nearly lost my hand. The bag bit me."

Lydia watched the crowbars appear with a bored expression, then smirked. "Finally. Someone else in this group might be fun." They all ignored her, which caused her to pout.

"How does it work?" Will asked, his eyes fixed on the bag. Kell let him hold it. It felt and looked like an empty bag.

"You stick your hand in the bag and grab an item," he instructed.

Will hesitated for a moment, wondering if it would bite him, then stuck his hand in. Nothing happened. He looked up at Kell with an eyebrow raised to see Kell's wide grin.

"The intent is the critical part. The bag has a sense of its owner somehow. If the owner wants to see an item, or all the items, they will see what they want if it's in there. It has come in handy on some of our heists because you can't get caught with the items."

"That is quite impressive," he said, then went back to his folders, which were now buried under Kell's supplies, as Dorna moved them to the counter.

He swept the rest of the dossiers into a pile, scanning the faces. The plan called for a minimum of five. They had only four, and with such a small number, no plan could guarantee they all came out alive. He eyed the door, wondering if he should risk a signal to the outside or wait for the last arrival to show.

"Anyone else coming?" he asked, but they only shrugged.

He pored over his files, racking his brain for ideas on how to get to the fifth floor of the Citadel past multiple guards, priestesses, and various protective measures, while Kell and Dorna built explosives.

Just as Will was sinking into the plans again, fingers brushed his shoulder, then shifted into a massage of his neck. Warm breath ghosted his ear, followed by lips.

He shut his eyes, inhaled once, then pushed her gently but firmly away.

"Lydia. I appreciate the offer, but I'm trying to work."

"I'm obviously a burden," she said, causing him to look up and notice she had changed into her regular clothing. "I'm going into town. I need a drink."

"We have supplies here," he replied evenly. "You'll have to pass the barriers again. Does that present a problem? Would you prefer an escort?"

"I don't want to take you from this vital work," she snapped. "I'll be fine. Just... make progress. I'll be at the closest tavern outside the stables."

The steel door clicked shut behind her.

Silence stretched.

Then Dorna muttered, deadpan, "Thank the gods. Her pacing was going to crack my skull."

He had been so engrossed in the other stuff that he hadn't even noticed.

"She's not all bad. We'll need someone creating chaos outside the Citadel when the time comes, and... chaos is her specialty," Will responded, turning back to his files.

Kell tapped a stylus against a detonator, eyeing the scattered dossiers. "Nothing against the three of us, but this job? With this roster? That's not a heist, it's a prayer request."

Will let his forehead rest against his palm. "I know. I'm all for suicidal odds, but right now this feels... pointless."

He felt like heading to the tavern for a drink himself, but he didn't want to spend more time with Lydia.

This felt pointless.

Kell stretched, bones cracking. "Dorna and I have been traveling for a couple of days straight. We have everything set up and prepared. We are going to rest for a bit. Let us know if there is something you need."

They walked hand in hand to the empty bedroom and closed the door, answering his other question about whether they were together.

CHAPTER 6 –
CALM BEFORE THE STORM

Will's focus shifted when the door opened without a knock or noise from the other side. Angel entered with the momentum of someone too busy for dramatics. She wore the robes of a high priestess, perfectly tailored, ceremonial sigils spotless, not a single thread out of place. Even Lydia, if she were here, would have admired the commitment to the bit. Angel's blue eyes swept the room, quick and surgical. She walked catlike inside with the confidence of someone who knew she was in charge.

He listened for sounds from the bedroom where Kell and Dorna were. Only the muffled snores of one of them rose through the door. Kell must have meant it when he said they were exhausted.

She carried two duffels. The bags were made of waxed canvas, their dull gray, reinforced seams hid whatever was inside. Each likely weighed more than Lydia, but she carried them with ease. Angel deposited them onto the steel table with a clatter and a grunt.

Will straightened from his slouch. The sight of Angel brought an odd relief like a condemned man seeing his executioner arrive on time. He managed a "Hey there," but Angel was already moving, opening the first duffel.

"Chase and Connelly said your pixie just left," Angel said without looking up. "You expect her back soon?"

Angel began digging through the bags.

Will's jaw flexed when he noticed that no one had followed her in. They needed more people for this heist, and as amazing as Angel was... They needed more. He hoped more were following her.

"Probably. She has the attention span of a gnat, and this place was a bit too focused for her."

He hesitated. "It's just us?" He hoped the others were on their way.

Angel paused in her inventory. "It is surprisingly challenging to recruit for suicide missions," she offered. "Where are Kell and Dorna?"

"They are sleeping. We can fill them in the morning," he said, motioning to the room with the closed door. "We'll have to sleep in shifts as there aren't enough beds."

To that, Angel just grunted.

"If the plan is to sneak in the front, our only hope is a lot more muscle or a full crew. Disabling security at the same time would take three teams. With this size group, we either give up or find an alternate way in." His gut wrenched with the realization that the likelihood of a suicide mission just went up. It was probably a better thing for Lydia not to be in the room anyway then.

He could hear her in his head: *"Can't spend the money from the job if we aren't alive to spend it."*

"Messy," Angel finished. "We'll make do. I did bring help, if not people."

She removed the two sets of priestess robes at the top of the bag, revealing a false bottom. When she opened that, she pulled out an array of gear: a nested bundle of security badges, a full mask respirator, and what looked like a fist-sized device with wires sprouting from its terminal.

Will whistled. "That's not standard issue."

Angel's mouth twitched, her version of a smile. She extracted the device and set it on the table. "Electro-magnetic pulse generator. Not a toy. It will fry their comms, doors, and internal security. It should provide us the time we need for a blackout before backup comes online."

Will leaned in, fingers twitching to touch. "You got an EMP? It looks heavy. How much does it weigh?"

"It's not bad," Angel said, "but it will need to be deployed in the middle of the Citadel before we get to the second floor or above. They have too much security technology to do the job without disabling it. Their sensors and cameras will be blind until they can find workarounds."

Will considered, then gestured at the second duffel. "What's in there? You didn't get your hands on a Kaltha staff. I thought we learned the hard way that using ancestral magical items was a bad thing when you aren't attuned." He joked, hoping that recalling one of their memorable assignments together would remind her how good they were together.

Angel's eyes flickered, and her face softened a touch. He could almost see the corners of her mouth rise. "This isn't the borderlands, and I did learn my lesson about the use of it, which is why I took a few years after learning about channeling ancestral magic." That comment took him by surprise. Ancestral magic was not easy to learn, as few tribes still practice it.

"The second bag has a magical Glyph lifted from an Alorian arms dealer last month. It cancels out their magical defenses. It's noisy, it's risky, and it's probably traceable. But it will give us a window without their wards, at least until they can find and destroy it. Hopefully, she can place it somewhere hidden, where they will have to look for it."

Will let out a low whistle. "That is not easy to obtain. The Resistance must really want this thing."

Angel gave him a dubious look as she pulled three additional uniforms out of her bag. "You're tall for a Votary, but they'll be on the lookout for out-of-uniform muscle. No one who values their life would dress as a Disciple."

"Except for the part where we're both on every watch list east of the Ridge," Will said.

Angel shrugged. "Don't you remember? You should be listed as 'presumed dead' in the Order's ledger thanks to that assignment you were on ten years ago, where only you and two others survived, but were reported dead. Use that to your advantage."

Will snorted, then caught himself, glancing at the door. "After this, that status may be the real one… and if they identify us, we can assume we have targets on our backs as well as any family or friends we have. The guards at the entrance, Chase and Connelly, could help. You trust them?"

Angel shook her head, short and sharp. "They already have their assignments. They will be placing distractions around town to pull as many guards away from the Citadel as possible. Their job is to stage a riot at the first sign of trouble. Lydia would be a good choice for that, as she will also be out of the main fire. I don't like having unknowns when I'm on an assignment. No one's coming to help us."

Will's stomach knotted. "So, it's really just the four of us going into the vault, then? You are the strategic genius, and it is only because it is your plan that I'll follow. As suicide missions go, this might be the least likely to succeed I've ever been part of."

She arched her eyebrow at him but didn't respond.

Will reached for the EMP device, hefting it and feeling its weight. It was cold and bulky, but Lydia should be able to lift it. The plan would be for her to carry both this and the glyph. He wondered how she would do with that.

Will stared at the empty square labeled "*vault*," tapping the table with slow, controlled frustration.

He set the EMP down. "You have a map of the vault?"

Angel's silent pause said enough before the words did. "Well. About that. I have schematics for most of the Citadel. I don't have details on the inside of the vault."

That did not sound like a yes.

"How in the hell are we supposed to plan if we don't know what we will face once we get inside?"

Angel hesitated. Just long enough for Will to catch it, small as a breath. "The Council claims this is all we have."

She unrolled a thick cluster of blueprints from the duffel and spread them across the table. The paper smelled of dust, ink, and secrecy. Will recognized the layout immediately: the Citadel of Eternal Vigil's inner sanctum. Every corridor. Every checkpoint. Every secured threshold was layered with glyphs and steel.

Angel tapped the sheet with a clipped, confident rhythm. "Three layers of security. Tech. Magic. Human. We neutralize the first two, and improvise with the third."

He held her gaze, but she didn't elaborate. Instead, she carefully rolled up the blueprints and leaned forward, her voice low and raw around the edges. "There is something you should know. My original team didn't make it past the river. Guards searched them and found weapons. They were shot on sight."

Will stilled.

Angel continued. "The second team made it farther. They got inside and even reached the second floor. The Order Guards and Priestesses overwhelmed them. They fight like trained executioners. Fast. United. Without hesitation."

The words sat between them like wet ash.

"Just a few can easily take out a squad. You can imagine what hundreds would be like."

The news hit Will like a physical blow, hollowing out his chest. His throat constricted as he forced out the words. "Anybody I know?"

"Harper. Esk. Trasker." Angel's voice remained flat, but her fingers tightened around the edge of the blueprint until her knuckles whitened. "A few others you'd recognize from the old days. All dead."

Will pressed a shaking hand through his hair. The overhead light flickered, throwing sharp shadows across his jaw. "So that's why you came yourself."

She nodded. The motion revealed a loose strand of dark hair that swept across her cheek, but she didn't bother tucking it back. "I trust you. You are predictable. You finish what needs doing. Lydia is good at what she does, but I will not rely on her for anything beyond chaos."

Will huffed a humorless breath. "She will be flattered, but you are right."

He began pacing, boots striking soft against stone. "So, best case scenario: we get in. Lydia sets off the EMP and kills the wards. We grab the tomes, then walk out dressed like them. Worst case: every alarm triggers and we end up decorative."

Angel's tone did not change. "Correct."

"They better be worth it. Are they truly that dangerous?"

Angel nodded. "Yes. And yes. This may shift the balance of power."

Will stopped pacing. "How do we get out after the vault?"

"Sources say that there might be hidden exits inside the vault itself. If not, there are access tunnels behind the reliquary that handle air, heat, and waste. We crawl down those and navigate back into the servant tunnels below. The route will be tight. You won't like it."

Will's jaw clenched. Confined spaces had never been his strength. She remembered.

He nodded anyway.

He turned back to Angel. "We should brief Lydia. She'll want to know what she's up against."

Angel studied him for a beat, something unreadable flickering across her expression. "She likes you, you know."

Will scoffed, unwilling to take the bait. "She likes chaos. I'm just convenient."

Angel smiled then, a small, tired thing that pulled faint color to her cheeks. "You're a little more than convenient, Will."

He ignored the warmth that tried to climb up his throat and reached for the EMP again. "Let's go through this from the beginning. Every step. Every contingency."

Angel didn't argue. She simply nodded and moved beside him.

For a brief moment, with blueprint ink under their fingers and danger closing in from every direction, Will remembered why he had followed her once.

Not because she commanded him.

Because she knew what needed to be done.

They continued working through every option and idea for thirty or forty minutes. They focused on possibilities, failures, and alternative approaches, each contributing to a detailed plan.

The plan was forming.

What remained was the part no blueprint could prepare them for.

All that remained was to survive it.

TOMES of MORETH

The sound of Lydia's boots in the corridor was his first warning. Heavy. Purposeful. Each step announced trouble long before she reached the door. She knocked once, then entered with a sweep of red hair and a scowl sharpened into a weapon. Will caught the door before it slammed and eased it shut.

She noticed Angel instantly.

Her eyes narrowed. The smile she offered could have cut bone.

"Well, look what the cat dragged in," she said, voice honeyed and venomous. She reeked of liquor. He was honestly surprised she'd made it past the pressure plates and dart traps.

Angel didn't look up. She acknowledged Lydia with a slight nod and kept reviewing the map.

The temperature in the room shifted, a silent current of hostility running between the two women, accentuated by Lydia's magical internal flames.

"We're just finishing up," Will offered, tone neutral.

Lydia's gaze flicked to the duffels, then to him. "Not enough beds," she observed. Her smirk grew. "Unless you two want to share."

Will exhaled through his nose. "There are mats under one of the beds. We rotate. Take it or leave it."

She ignored the response and leaned against the wall, arms crossed, chin lifted in challenge.

"Those guards at the entrance are so sweet... and so big. They helped me down here."

"Chase and Connelly are good at their jobs," Angel responded without raising her eyes.

Lydia crossed the room and grabbed Will's arm. "I'm taking my man to bed."

She pulled, but Will didn't move a fraction.

Angel didn't comment. She just murmured, "If you want to sleep, Will, go. I'll be here while finding whatever we're still missing."

There was no accusation in her tone. That almost made it worse.

Something ugly flickered in Lydia's expression. She slipped toward the bedroom door, dragging her fingers along the wall in a trail of impatience. "We need to talk. Alone."

He followed her to the bedroom, not because he wanted to, but because he knew there was no point in resisting.

Lydia shut the door behind them with the deliberate slowness of someone about to start a fight.

She went straight for him, hands on his shirt, pushing him against the wall. The move was practiced, more muscle memory than seduction, and he didn't react.

When she realized, she said, "You really going through with this? It isn't going to end well," and she whispered, pressing her body against his.

Will didn't move. He kept his hands at his sides, letting her do what she thought she needed.

"We don't have a choice." His voice was quiet. Controlled. Too controlled.

He guided her back, not rough, but firm.

Lydia bit her lip in frustration. "You could say no. We could leave and go back to having fun."

He looked at her, really looked, and saw the panic behind the bravado. "I'm not leaving them to do it alone. You would be safer if you decided not to do this. I could get you some coin and you could head out and settle yourself somewhere far from here," he said, hoping she would take him up on the offer. They could find someone else to be their distraction.

She laughed, sharp and bitter. Then, she tried to kiss him, but he turned his head away.

Lydia froze, then pulled back. She searched his face for the reason.

He spoke softly, but the words landed with finality. "I need to get back to planning if I want any of us to survive."

For a second, her face blanked. She had no script for this. He had never turned her down. She went from zero to fury in the space of a breath. "Oh, I see. You have a thing for ice queens now." She shoved him, hard enough that he almost stumbled.

He righted himself, jaw clenched. "Grow up."

She stamped her foot, full tantrum. "Don't talk to me like I'm a kid."

"Then stop acting like one." His voice was cool and even.

Will opened the door and stepped outside, intending to leave her with her anger. She slammed it back with enough force to rattle the hinges. "Fine then," she yelled, her voice raw.

He stared at the closed door for a moment and waited to hear the expected sound of items crashing against the walls. He rolled his eyes when it came.

He said nothing. There was nothing to say. The snoring had stopped in the other room, but they didn't come out.

Will turned around to face Angel, who had been motionless and silent. He felt like he'd just run ten blocks through the rain. Angel glanced up, took in his expression, and said nothing. She slid a mug of tea across the table toward him.

He ignored it, sitting at the far end, eyes on the blueprints but not seeing them. The air in the safehouse pressed inward, too tight, too stale, and too small.

He needed air. He needed out.

He muttered, "Going for a walk." Then he walked out before anyone could stop him.

Outside, rain had started; thick, cold drops hammered stone and skin in the same rhythm. Will hunched his shoulders and walked, letting the chill numb his face and letting the city swallow his thoughts.

He kept walking, through alleys and market streets, until he found a tavern. It was nearly empty. He slid into a corner booth, ordered a drink, and nursed it, watching the reflections of the streetlights in puddles outside.

The city was alive, even at this hour. He could hear the distant bells, the shouts of drunks, and the low hum of magic. It felt safe, in a strange way, as if by sitting there long enough, the rest of the world would fix itself.

Will nursed his third drink, staring through the rain-streaked glass at the warped, watery mirror of the city outside. He'd chosen the darkest booth in the tavern, tucked so far into the corner it almost felt like a confession box.

For the first time in days, Will let his mind drift, blank and weightless.

He felt a light touch on his shoulder.

His muscles coiled. The knife beneath his shirt was halfway free before a calm voice cut through his trigger reflex.

"It's just me," Angel said in a calm, casual tone.

Will exhaled.

She slid into the bench across from him, moving with the confident grace of someone who'd spent half her life ducking bullets and the other half shooting bullets for other people to duck.

She flagged the bartender with a nod, then looked Will over as if performing triage. "You must have been deep in thought if I surprised you. I figured you would have seen me walk in."

Will grunted. "That would be an understatement."

Angel studied him for a moment. The bartender dropped a bottle and two glasses on the table. She poured, her movements clean and efficient, then took a measured sip and asked, "You all right?"

Will rolled the glass in his hand, watching the way it caught the light. "You didn't come here to talk feelings."

Angel's mouth twitched. "Maybe I wanted company."

He snorted. "You hate company. You were very clear that we were associates and nothing more when we parted ways all those years ago."

Angel shrugged one shoulder, eyes never leaving his. "People change."

They sat in silence, the only sound was the distant rain and the slow, deliberate cleaning of glasses behind the bar.

Will took a long pull, savoring the burn as it went down.

Angel set her glass down. "Remember when you rigged the bell at school?"

Will's jaw relaxed, just barely. "It played that song for a week. They couldn't get it to stop. The headmaster nearly lost his damn mind, but they could never pin it on me."

"They tried, though." Angel leaned in, elbows on the table. "You rewired the whole system in under an hour. People said it was magic."

Will huffed a laugh. "Only because they didn't know you stole the custodian's keys and locked him in the supply closet."

Angel's blue eyes glinted. "We did have some fun back then."

Will felt a strange warmth wash over him as he sank back into his memories. "High school had its good times and its bad."

Angel traced the rim of her glass with one fingertip. "At first, I didn't like you."

Will raised an eyebrow. "Oh, I remember."

She met his gaze, steady. "I respected you at first. You were that scrawny kid who never really got along with the rest of them. You were quiet, angry, and brilliant. I was at a point where I was trying to fit in with the rest of them. I couldn't like you at first. There's a difference."

The bartender came by with fresh drinks.

He looked at her, seeing the lines that hadn't been there in high school, the small scar under her jaw, the way her hands always moved, restless, never at peace. "That's not how I remember it."

Angel's voice softened, just a little. "How do you remember it, Will?"

He shook his head. "I remember that school dance. Tommy Kiswit was being a jerk to you, like he was to everyone. When I saw him and his friends trying to attack you in the hall at the dance... I straightened him out, then we danced. You were my first kiss."

Angel reached across the table, her fingers brushing his wrist. "I remember. We were inseparable after that. For years."

He froze, unsure whether to pull away or not. The contact felt electric.

She didn't let go. "You ever wonder what would've happened if we'd..."

Will cut her off, not unkindly. "No. I don't."

Angel's smile turned sad. "Liar."

He drained his glass, then set it down with a clink. "What's the play here, Angel? You left me. You told me that we were through... for the good of the Resistance. We both had our roles to play, and after all those years, I didn't fit into yours. You want to walk down memory lane, or are you just killing time before we all get killed?"

Angel leaned back, watching him. "We're not all going to die."

Will laughed, low and bitter. "Now who's the liar?"

Angel's gaze went somewhere distant. "You're right. But I want you to know that if we don't make it, I'm glad it's you and me. Not anyone else."

Will felt the words land, heavy and hot. He looked away at the window, at the rain. He didn't know what to do with that kind of honesty.

He heard the chair scrape but kept his head down, focusing on his glass. He felt Angel's hand again, this time warmer, more deliberate. She had moved closer, beside him.

He wanted to kiss her. He could feel the moment, the gravity of it. He wanted it badly. Then he thought of Lydia. Yes. She had likely slept with multiple people while she was out, but... that didn't mean it was right, and he wasn't going to do that.

Instead, he pulled away, abrupt, nearly spilling the drink. "I should get back."

Angel blinked, hurt flickering over her face before she buried it. "Of course."

Will stood, fumbling for coins, then stopped. "I'm sorry," he said, meaning it.

Angel nodded, finishing her drink in one swallow. "Go."

Something inside him twisted with a nameless feeling of regret, anger, and longing. He only knew it hurt.

He left, with the door banging behind him, rain cold on his face. He walked the city in circles, his thoughts buzzing with regret, confusion, and longing.

The rain washed the city, but not him.

By the time he reached the safehouse, his shoes squelched and his hands shook.

Angel was in the main room, reading by the dim light, her expression neutral. She didn't look up.

He went into the room where Lydia was. She was sound asleep, snoring on the bed. He changed into dry clothes, pulled out an extra blanket from his pack, and found a spot on the floor out of the way to close his eyes.

He didn't know what would happen next. Maybe nothing. Maybe everything.

He waited for the world to start moving again.

Chapter 7 –
Never Be Prepared Enough

Will assessed the blueprints before him, using random objects from the room arranged by Angel to act as their avatars. He pondered her choice of a rock for him. She had given Lydia a scorched matchstick, at least that one was obvious. She gave herself a pen cap, and the small spice shakers represented Dorna and Kell positioned side by side.

The safehouse war room was a tomb at this after-dawn hour, with the lights dimmed and the concrete walls radiating a chill from a cold front that had passed through the night. A battered analog timer sat at one end, its thick second hand clicking with the confidence of a firing squad. It was loud enough that every click felt like a countdown to someone's death.

Lydia lounged two chairs down, arms thrown wide: her body language both open and predatory. She had spent most of the morning complaining about one thing or another.

Kell stooped, distracted by the contents of his endless bag, and Dorna in a sleeveless shirt that made her look even more like a walking siege engine. They took the seats opposite Will, barely glancing at him. He appreciated their social mercy. His patience was on edge.

Angel paced around the table. She reached for the timer, twisting the dial until it clicked fifteen minutes forward.

"This timer is how much time we can realistically expect before the magic wards come back up. We have one shot. We will run through this on paper until everyone knows when and where they should be," Angel said, tapping the pen cap avatar. "No reinforcements. No comms. If you trip an alarm, you trigger the Citadel's full lockdown. That means gas, magic wards, and so many versions of kill teams we don't even know them all. There's no overtime. If you're late, you're dead."

She slid a hand over the blueprints, smoothing out a crease that bisected the inner sanctum. "First priority is the vault. It's here, on the top floor, with protection of all kinds. We will need to be prepared with extra charges while we are inside. They will be needed for the escape." She nodded at Dorna.

Dorna produced a bag full of pastel blue putty, a bag of balls, a pile of thin sheets, and a row of syringes. "The beauty of these is that they use a physical trigger. The putty goes down first, then I add the ball. It has a gel coating that will dissolve. I'm going to set them. There will be pros and cons to this, though. The bombs will go off, but they will help us escape. We need to make sure not to go back the way we came. When they go off, it will be loud, so only use it when needed."

She looked at each member in turn. "If you want to keep all your fingers, don't touch the gel."

Kell snorted. "Even better. If you want something to boom faster… You just need to break the gel… and BOOM!"

Angel ignored him. She took out four tiny earbuds and dropped them into the center of the table. "Comms, but only in emergencies. They work off something similar to humm worms and can transmit even after the EMP and glyph. We don't know how, but the Order can hear them. Only use them if you need to warn the team, you get one second before you're compromised."

Lydia flicked her matchstick at the earbuds. "They don't climb into my ears like the humm worms, do they? How will I know when you need the distraction?"

"No. These aren't permanent translators like the humm worms, so they only need to sit in your ear. As far as when… You should hear us trying to leave." Although she was likely irritated with Lydia… they all were… she responded calmly. Lydia had not liked having the translator placed in her when they left the city. The idea that a little worm lived in your inner ear was a bit difficult to accept for most. Her control was quite impressive.

Angel continued, "The critical path is here." She moved the pen cap from the north wall to the center vault. "We have fifteen minutes between setting it off and their being able to restart it. We don't know how long it will take them to realize that it is down. If they start while we are in the vault, we won't be able to walk down those halls on the vault floor; our only hope will be to get out of the vault another way."

"Once Lydia triggers the EMP and disables the magical ward, we grab the Tomes from the vault before they can raise the wards, then leave. If possible, we will head back down the tunnels and get out safely, but since the bombs will be triggering, we will only go that way if we don't have any other options."

"The backup plan is, we will separate and blend in with the guards, then meet at the rendezvous location outside of town." She stopped to look at each of them, then added, "It is a risky plan, but vital. These Tomes could be the answer to allowing people with magic to no longer risk death from technology. This could save those with magic within Media."

Kell looked up from his bag, eyes sharp for the first time. "Dorna and I have family in Media that need this. It could be a suicide mission, but we are in it to the end. Do we know more details about the lock on the vault door?"

Angel handed him a folder. "Here is what we have. Disabling it is your responsibility. You're the only one with experience to disarm it."

Kell considered, then went back to fiddling with a roll of copper tape. "How many guards will we need to pass to get in? If they upped security since the last pass, we're all screwed."

Will answered because he was the only one who'd memorized the schedule. "Obviously, we don't know what to expect on the inside, but as far as the gates, we are dealing with eight on shift, six overnight. There will be two patrols on the outer ring, two at the gate. The rest rotate inside. One Disciple is equal to three or four typical Media guards. They have spent years studying and focusing on how to kill."

"So, like you," Lydia piped up.

"Yes. Like me, but with a dedication to death that even I don't have," he said.

He continued, "They do a shift change at five bells, which means they're on high alert with both shifts on site, so we must wait until the first shift leaves. At six bells, it is the only opportunity we have on the fourth floor. Integration of a guard helped to fill in some additional details about the higher levels. There is a laser grid system that is a closed circuit in the hallways. We can't get through the halls to get to the vault doors unless we use that EMP. It is big enough that it will disrupt the whole building. If Lydia can't get the devices set and triggered, we are dead."

"I can do it," she said with a bravado she hadn't earned. He eyed her warily, to which she added, "I can. I need to place them and push a button on each. It's not THAT hard." He would probably pay for questioning her abilities, but it was that important.

At her response, the room fell silent.

Once the silence had settled, Angel addressed Will directly. "We'll be in the access tunnels for a while, as we should get into position on the floor when the six bells start. Will that still be a problem?"

He knew she was referring to the time in high school. That was years ago, and he still wasn't a fan of tight spaces.

He fought the urge to grind his teeth. "I can do it. I'm fine," Will snapped, then regretted it. "I'm fine." This time with more control and calm. Just thoughts of being back in that situation brought a slight sweat to his brow.

Lydia smirked, her voice a low purr. "He's fine, Love."

Dorna looked at Will, deadpan. "You're claustrophobic?"

Will managed, "Only if I'm conscious," which got a laugh from Kell and, begrudgingly, from Dorna.

Angel was unmoved. "If you lose it in the tunnels, we all die. There's no margin for error. Just in case, I'm preparing some practice, so we can know what we are dealing with ahead of time."

Will kept his eyes on the rock in front of him. "Noted." He couldn't let them down for this. He would have to get a handle on it.

Angel let it go. She rested her hand on the timer. "We are going to walk through this step by step, at the right time. We do it on paper to ensure everyone is on the same page and that we have the timing right. We have to memorize every turn." She tapped the blueprints. "I want you all to walk through it.

Eyes closed. Twice. Ready?" She flipped the timer's switch, starting it. "Go."

They ran through so many scenarios, with Angel throwing potential risks or flaws into each one. Each person stated where they would be and when they would take an action, until they felt confident that they had solutions to a majority of the challenges that could come up. After a full day of this, they had walked through and had things sounding solid.

Angel looked at the team, blue eyes as cold and clear as the room itself. "We get this done, we walk away knowing this may be the only way to save lives. Media now has a new technology that is no longer a chip inserted into people. It is a wide area frequency, and it will kill anyone with magic. These Tomes have the answers we need to counteract that technology. Understood?"

Everyone nodded.

No one spoke the obvious truth: nodding was easy. Surviving would be harder.

She dismissed them for a five-minute break. Kell and Dorna stepped out to get fresh air. Lydia followed them, trailing her fingers over his shoulder as she passed. He didn't flinch, but something in his spine recoiled anyway.

Angel waited for the room to clear. When they were alone, she asked, "You sure you can do this?"

Will didn't answer at first. He traced the grain of the table, then looked up, meeting her gaze. "I'm sure."

"I'm sorry for bringing it up, but..."

"I know. That was so long ago. I'm not a puny kid anymore, being picked on by older, bigger jerks."

She nodded once, almost imperceptibly. "Good. Because I need you at your best. Not for me. For them."

He tried to muster a smile, but the effort failed halfway. "I'll manage." He wasn't sure he would be able to manage, but it felt better to say he would.

Angel walked into the bedroom, closing the door behind her.

Will stayed in his seat, the ticking of the timer the only proof the world was still moving.

Chase and Connelly had built a makeshift tunnel system inside a warehouse at the edge of town. The building had once been part of a sprawling industrial plant. Now, only a scorched brick skeleton remained. Inside those bones, they had constructed a mock labyrinth. Angel had scouted it weeks ago to ensure it wasn't being used. They had built a maze of wooden walls, forming cramped crawl spaces, junctions, choke points, and dead ends designed to mimic the Citadel's inner maintenance corridors.

His brows drew together as he surveyed the structure, thoughts of climbing into the crawlspaces making his neck stiff and his palms sweat. He might not be a kid any longer, but he was also a much larger man than he was before, so it was much easier to get stuck in the small passages. He had been in tight spaces since, but it didn't make them any easier, and he had never stayed in one as long as he would be in these.

The factory's rusted smokestacks loomed like blackened sentinels against the dawn. The front gate hung crooked on a single hinge, screeching in protest when they pushed it aside. Lydia walked beside him with an almost eager bounce in her step, the cold air turning her breath into white vapor. Dorna and Kell trailed, both silent, perhaps regretting the night's lack of sleep or the early call time.

They descended to the basement level loading pit, where a dark opening waited in the wall. It was barely large enough for a grown person to squeeze into.

Angel gathered them at the entrance.

"This is the layout," she said. "One simulated floor, from the hatch to the vault corridor. Four turns. One choke point.

These tunnels are tighter than the real ones, so if you can make it here, you can make it in the Citadel."

Will felt the weight of her last sentence settle squarely on him. Maybe he imagined the extra second of eye contact. Maybe not.

Angel handed Lydia a stopwatch.

"You're not going through, so you're the timekeeper. You set the pace." Then she pointed. "Kell first. He'll clear traps and sensors. Dorna follows. Will and I will go next. Move."

Though his mind was screaming, no one argued.

Kell clicked a headlamp on, muttered a quick prayer to a god known only to thieves, and crouched into the tunnel. Dorna went behind him, movements steady and practiced. When Angel entered, every one of her movements was efficient, and she used no wasted words.

Will swallowed. The opening waited. The stale, cold air smelled like dust and old metal, the same smell every enclosed space carried in his memory.

Just move.

He lowered himself and slid forward onto his forearms.

The walls closed around him.

The place was worse than Will had imagined. Damp air pooled, and the only light came from the hissing battery lanterns Angel had mounted at key junctions. Even so, most of the corridors were bathed in near-blackness, and the walls closed in like the lid of a casket.

The opening was barely wide enough for his muscled shoulders. The rough walls dragged along his arms as he crawled, scraping his elbows each time he shifted his weight.

Left. Straight. Right.

His mind repeated the route like a rhyme.

Squeeze under the pipe.

Keep going.

But after the first turn, his hands began to tremble.

His memories returned him to that small box he was shoved into in high school, when he was only an undersized first-year student in Media.

He heard Angel ahead of him. "Keep moving."

Again, he tried to focus on the route: left, straight, right, squeeze under the low pipe, keep going. But after the first turn, his hands were still trembling.

He heard Angel's voice ahead of him, "Keep moving," but her voice sounded far away.

Her voice steadied him, just as it had when he heard her while he was still in the box. She was the only one who had bothered to look for him back then, when everyone else walked away or laughed. She had listened, then acted. The only person who had pulled him out, handed him a towel, and walked him to Lysa's door with fury cold enough to burn. She was the only one who knew he had grown up in the Talvi slums.

She had been dating the jerk responsible when she heard them gloating about the punishment they had given him.

That wasn't when they became friends.

That came later.

Will tried to push onward, dragging his body with the strength of anger alone, but his head filled with static, and his vision narrowed to a tunnel of nothing but black. His breath turned shallow, sharp, useless.

On the second turn, he felt pressure on his chest. He couldn't breathe. He couldn't move. The walls leaned in, crushing his ribs, his spine, his throat. He started panting loudly and desperately.

He froze.

Somewhere, far away, Lydia laughed. Her laughter echoed through the void. It was a bright, careless sound that didn't belong in the dark. It made everything worse.

He inched backward toward the entrance, scraping his elbows raw. His knees and forearms scrambled for purchase, retreating blind, desperate, instinctive.

He couldn't finish.

He twisted and thrashed until he tumbled out of the tunnel's mouth and hit the floor. Hard.

He curled there, cheek pressed to the damp cement. His chest heaved. His fists shook against the ground as if trying to hold himself still. Sweat slicked his face, and his pulse hammered like a trapped animal.

Angel stood over him, unreadable. For a heartbeat, it was high school all over again. He could see her silhouette above him, the same as the day she had opened the box.

"You want to try again?" she asked, voice level, "or should we call it off? If you can't get through the tunnels, the mission fails. We need to know now."

Will glared at her, anger drowning shame.

"I'll do it," he breathed. "I need a break first."

Angel nodded once. "Five minutes. Then again." She turned to the others. "Everyone else, go through again. You still aren't fast enough."

Will stayed where he had fallen and stared up at the ruined rafters overhead. His pulse finally slowed, but the humiliation stayed sharp beneath his skin. He tried to remember the last time he had felt so naked, so entirely at the mercy of something he could neither stab nor reason with.

Footsteps approached.

Lydia crouched beside him, amusement curled at the edges of her voice. "Thought you said you were fine."

He considered lashing out, but there was no point. He ignored her.

Lydia shrugged and moved to her vantage point at the finish above, her banter with Kell carrying through the tunnels like a dare. Kell and Dorna stepped over him and climbed back into the tunnel.

When he caught his breath again, he stood and staggered out of the building, letting cold air bite his lungs clean.

Angel followed soundlessly until she was close enough to touch his arm gently.

"You're still in that moment," she said quietly. "But it's the past. You're not that boy anymore."

He refused to answer.

Angel didn't press. She simply stood beside him, letting silence make space instead of pressure.

Finally, Will whispered, "I know what I'm supposed to do. My body doesn't care."

Angel's response was soft but precise. "This isn't the same as last time."

He almost laughed, the sound brittle. "That's not how it feels."

Angel looked away, then she added, "Remember Kiswit?"

He did. He remembered everything about Tommy Kiswit, from the smug grin to the reek of his gym bag. He was the leader of the bullies responsible for this torture, which he was still in. Responsible for locking him in a box only large enough for him to sit in a ball, and not enough air holes to get enough air to breathe. It was four hours of absolute dark, and the panic was so absolute he'd pissed himself by hour two, though passing out from lack of oxygen had helped him forget some of the torture.

When Angel had rescued him, she had lived up to her name, and he had fallen for her immediately. Two weeks later, he remembered the way it ended: the blood on Tommy's face, the choking sound as he crushed the other boy's windpipe with both hands. It had been his first kill, if only he had gotten there before Tommy had attacked Angel in retribution.

"You killed Tommy, Will," Angel said softly. "You killed him, and you survived."

He closed his eyes. "I was fourteen."

Angel didn't offer pity, only facts. "He and his friends were seventeen and bigger. You survived."

He sat up and wiped his face with the back of his hand. "You have a point?" The frustration in his voice wasn't aimed at her. Not really.

He hated that his body still remembered fear better than logic.

Angel straightened and dusted off her knees. "Point is, you get through the tunnel. One way or another. And when it's over, you're still you. These tunnels have plenty of air, you can get out if you need to, and I will be ahead of you the whole time."

He tried to laugh, but it stuck. "You always did know how to motivate."

He forced a smirk. Humor was easier than honesty.

"Besides... the promise of staring at your ass every time I panic is a hell of a carrot."

Angel offered him her hand. He took it, surprised at how firm her grip was. She pulled him to his feet. "You are lucky I need you for this job after a comment like that." She said it with ferocity, but he noticed a tug of a smile on her lips.

"Ready?" she asked.

"No," he said. "But I'm going anyway."

She stepped into the tunnel and began to climb.

He stepped to the tunnel entrance, pushing through the blackness, meter by meter, counting each step. His skin crawled, sweat pooling at the small of his back, but he didn't stop.

When he reached the end, there was no applause, only the muffled sound of Dorna cursing in the crawlspace and the slow tick of the stopwatch. He lay there for a minute, catching his breath, then he crawled back to do it again.

They ran the drill six more times before noon. By the end, Will's shirt was translucent with sweat, and his knees were raw, but he knew every turn by heart. He stopped thinking about Kiswit. He stopped thinking about anything except the need to reach the other side.

Angel watched him on the last run, arms folded. "Not bad." Will nodded, throat too tight for words.

Angel turned to the rest of the team, who were sprawled on the floor, equally exhausted. "This is the easy part," she said. "In the real Citadel, you have three more floors, can't make as much noise, three checkpoints, and the risk of traps that we are not aware of. With all of us together, if you choke, you kill us all."

Dorna grunted. "No pressure."

Angel ignored her. "Eat, hydrate, recover. If you're not ready, you stay behind."

He wasn't ready. He doubted he ever would be.

But he'd go anyway.

CHAPTER 8 – MISSION PREP

Will woke before dawn and watched the haze crawl along the gutters, carrying the chill up through the cracks in the safehouse floor. He dressed, buttoned his shirt, laced his boots, and tried not to think about what would happen if the multitude of things that must occur couldn't.

The city lay under a dome of fog, every edge softened, every sound muffled. Luckily, Lydia was still sleeping. He had used exhaustion as the reason for not having sex last night, but he knew that would not be good enough this morning, so he attempted to leave before she woke.

They spent the day running the final tests.

Dorna and Kell set out first, splitting off with duffel bags to plant the test charges at predetermined checkpoints around the perimeter. Kell, being the consummate thief, had an eye for rhythm and routine; he was cautious, always watching for the telltale shuffle of security patrols, always finding new ways to make himself invisible.

Dorna, by contrast, moved through the world as if it owed her safe passage, and it was a rarity if people stopped her, not even when she walked with a bag of explosives on her back. She had perfected the higher-level priestess walk, walking with authority and control.

Lydia's challenge for the day was to run her route solo. She had to reach the middle of the lowest tier of the Citadel undetected and make it back to the street in under eight minutes. She had been practicing how to adjust her swaying hips so that she would look more like the assassin priestesses and less like her seductive self. She had improved, though she slipped regularly.

Although she was supposed to perform alone, Will shadowed her, ready to provide backup if needed. He watched her from the shadows as she slid past a pair of Votaries, then walked straight through the main entrance of the Citadel and into the main chapel. Her pace never faltered. Every motion was smooth, calculated, and feline.

A Disciple at the corner lifted his head, gaze sliding over her like a blade searching for a flaw.

Will braced, ready to step out, ready to kill.

But the guard looked away.

Lydia continued without hesitation.

She performed flawlessly and didn't get stopped by anyone.

As he silently applauded her success from a distance, a voice barked behind him. "What are you doing there? Your markings are Shadow troupe. They are in prayer now. Why are you not with them?"

He turned, already running a cover story through his head, but then he noticed the guard was in an officer's uniform with silver honor cords, every inch regulation. They were the deadliest and fully devoted to Tamris. He paused and cleared his throat.

"I asked what you're doing," he said, one hand on his sidearm.

"The Word is Law; the Law is Light. Sorry, sir. My Votary asked me to deliver a message," Will lied. "My hands serve where Tamris commands; my heart serves where Tamris wills," he said, repeating the words he knew were expected of a devotee.

He squinted, distrustful. "Show me your work order."

Will reached for his pocket, stalling, scanning for exits. He could see the story breaking down in his eyes, anticipating the moment when he would call his bluff.

Will had his hand on the hilt of the hidden knife, about to pull it out, when he heard her speak behind him. "Problem, Votary?" Angel said, voice sharp as a scalpel. "You were instructed to deliver that message by your Acolyte. The Templar is waiting for it." Her tone made Will flinch, and he found her very believable.

He hoped the guard would agree. Her genius was undeniable. The Templar was not someone you wanted to have an audience with for any reason, much less to deliver bad news. He was violence incarnate.

He turned to face her and found her perfectly fitting the part of a Third-level High Priestess. She radiated authority so purely that the guard snapped to attention without thinking.

"He is with you?" the guard asked, with a pause.

"He is, and his message is urgent. I assume you had a good reason for stopping him. I will ensure that information gets back to his Acolyte. This will earn him extra training in the ring for any delays."

The Votary stepped back and placed both hands steepled in front of his face as a sign of submission to her. Angel's plan was working. Will steepled his hands also, adding a slight bow to his head.

The guard stammered, "Please do, High Luminary. This man was..."

Angel cut him off with a gesture. "He will pay for his insolence. We are expected. May the Vigil find you sharp, and the Word guide your steps." With these words, she walked away, and Will followed dutifully behind her.

When Will glanced back, the guard paled and retreated up the corridor.

Angel waited until they were completely alone, then stopped, turned, and looked at Will. "I did not expect to need to save you today. How many times have I saved you now?"

"I am fairly sure the score is even now," he said, with a wink and a crooked grin.

"Ha! You wish."

He opened his mouth to protest, but she silenced him with a look and added, "Don't let it happen tomorrow."

Will exhaled slowly. His palms were damp. Too close.

"The pixie managed her part without incident. I was surprised," Will said.

"More than I can say for you," she chided with a raised eyebrow, as she walked off, her steps echoing like gunshots in the empty corridor.

By evening, the team reconvened at a tavern near the safehouse. It was a local favorite and lively. A band in the corner played songs about bad decisions and worse lovers. Angel assured them the owners were not loyal to the Order. That was the only reason any of them were here.

Dorna and Kell had already demolished a plate of fried vegetables, and Lydia was halfway through her second bottle of cider, cheeks flushed and posture loose.

Will slid into the booth beside her. She looped her arm through his and nuzzled his shoulder, more tactile than usual. He let her. He wasn't sure whether it irritated him or comforted him. The truth sat heavy in him: there was a good chance he'd be dead tomorrow, and Lydia needed to believe she mattered to him so she would perform her part. With the chill in the air, her warmth was welcome, even if he didn't have any feelings behind it.

Angel arrived last.

She moved like someone whose mind was already three steps ahead. She slid into the seat across from Will. She didn't order. She didn't smile. She stared at the center of the table as if it held the answer to a question she couldn't allow herself to ask out loud.

For a long while, no one spoke. The silence was swallowed by laughter from nearby tables and the pounding rhythm of the band playing raunchy songs that encouraged dancing and fun.

Finally, Lydia broke the silence. "You think we're ready?"

Kell barked a laugh, humor sharp as a blade. "Ready as we're ever going to be."

Dorna only grunted, lifting her third beer in a humorless toast.

"Pir-Slaint!" Her use of the traditional Elven toast seemed perfect for the occasion.

Everyone raised their glasses in agreement and parroted the toast.

When the positive vibes had calmed, Angel looked at Will, her blue eyes unreadable. "You set?"

He nodded, then realized he hadn't spoken aloud. "Yeah," he said quietly. "I'm set."

Lydia squeezed his arm, her grip almost painful. "We're gonna be legends," she said, almost reverent. "People will tell stories about this job for decades."

Will looked at her, with her bright hair and reckless confidence. He owed her the truth.

"No," he said softly. "If we're lucky, no one will know it was us. We want this forgotten, not famous. In fact, if they get their hands on any one of us, they might be able to get the others' names. The moment the Order has people to pin to the heist on, they'll hunt down everyone we've ever cared about and burn every trace of us off the map."

His words were sobering.

It lingered throughout the rest of the meal. Through the drinks. Through the motions of pretending they were normal people eating a regular dinner.

Eventually, Dorna and Kell drifted out. This might be their last night together, so when they left for the safehouse, he wanted to give them space. As they walked out, he saw that a rainstorm had started outside. Thunder rolled after them like a warning.

He had noticed Lydia flirting with the barmaid between bites. She got up to powder her nose. On her way back, she walked up to her for a long conversation, while Angel and he sat in silence. He kept glancing up at Lydia, but he wasn't concerned about what she was doing.

Maybe she was getting the hint that he wasn't available to meet her sexual needs and was going elsewhere.

Lydia walked up to him, a young barmaid on her arm.

"My new friend wants to have some fun," she said lightly. "She's not into you, but... You don't mind if I step away for a while, do you?"

Will swallowed his fourth drink and set the glass down with more finality than he intended.

"You enjoy yourself," he said. "Tonight, might be the last chance any of us get. And I know I'm not in an enjoyment mood right now."

Lydia giggled, kissed the barmaid's throat in plain view of half the tavern, then followed her upstairs to the rooms above the inn.

He didn't watch them go, but the sound of her laughter disappearing up the stairs settled in his chest like a weight.

When she was gone, Angel caught his eye and spoke, "Looks like you have an interesting relationship with her."

"I was about to leave her, but… she's not all bad; she's just not good for me. I was going to break up with her, then I found out about this job and selfishly thought it would be better if I were at least doing something that meant something. That hasn't worked either. Why break up with her… if I'm going to die tomorrow?"

Angel reached over the table to meet his hand. Her touch felt like a shock of life to his system. "If we make it out, what do you want to do?"

He watched the rain through the small window. "I haven't thought that far ahead."

Angel smiled, soft and sad. "Liar."

He closed his eyes and listened to the storm rage. He tried not to think of the tunnels, or the vault, or the feeling of Angel's hand on his.

Tomorrow at six bells, Lydia would need to hit both triggers, or they all would die. He put his trust in her to do it.

He just didn't know if he trusted himself.

The band kept playing, and the rain kept falling. The night held its breath, waiting for what came next.

Angel moved to sit next to him. The electric feel of her body so near to his stirred something in him. He closed his eyes, fearing he would see pity in her eyes.

"Come dance with me. Like old times," she instructed, turning his face to hers. He opened his eyes to see a warmth and desire in her eyes he hadn't seen in years, then he felt her pulling him up from the seat.

He knew he shouldn't. He hadn't officially broken up with Lydia. She might sleep with others, but it didn't feel right to do that to her. Tonight might be his last night alive, and if it was, Angel was who he wanted to spend it with. She was asking him to dance. How would he feel if he denied her this simple request? He complied and followed her out to the dance floor, where a slow song had started.

He wrapped his arms around her, her head resting comfortably on his chest. It brought him back to that school dance, their first kiss, and what happened later that night. Holding her close, the aroma of spices and vanilla mixed with the ale around them.

Lost in the music and memories, he looked down to see her staring up at him. She reached up to touch his face, then pulled him down to hers into a kiss. Her lips felt soft and searching as her arms moved around his neck, pulling him closer. His arms moved around her small waist, his fingers caressing the dip in her lower back.

It started tender and searching, then he felt the fire of unsaid feelings bloom between them, and it deepened as her lips parted, giving him access to explore.

The tavern's pulsing bassline throbbed, providing a primal rhythm that synced with the frantic beat of their hearts. He was lost in the haze of the drinks and her scent.

Her body moved like a symphony of sin against him, her hips pushed against him, grinding with need.

She grabbed his face before crashing her lips into his. It was hard to call it a kiss; it was so ferocious. Her tongue plunged into his mouth, hot and demanding, making him groan. His hands gripped her hips like they were the only thing keeping him grounded.

Her taste was intoxicating, and he returned her kiss with equal fervor. The heat between them was like fucking wildfire.

Without warning, she grabbed his wrist and dragged him toward the bathroom.

He barely got to the entrance before she pulled him inside and slammed the door shut, twisting the lock with a smirk that could've brought a lesser man to their knees.

The tiny bathroom reeked of stale piss and cheap disinfectant, but neither of them gave a fuck. She pressed him against the sink, her body grinding against his with a ferocity that made his cock throb against the confines of his jeans. Her hands were everywhere. She tugged at his shirt, raking through his hair, palming the hard bulge in his pants with a grin that screamed trouble.

"Fuck me," she whispered, her voice a husky command that shot straight to his groin. A fleeting thought of Lydia flashed through his mind, but Angel was here. Angel was the one he had wanted all along, and she wanted him. There was no Lydia after this.

It wasn't that he didn't know better.

It was that, for once in his life, he let want win over survival.

He didn't need to be told twice.

She was already unbuttoning her pants, so he worked on his own, then opened her shirt to reveal her perfect breasts. He spun her around, pinning her to the grimy sink with a growl, enjoying the view in the mirror above the sink. One hand firmly gripping her left breast, while his other hand reached in front of her between her legs. She moaned when he slipped inside her moist folds, arching into him. She was dripping, slick and inviting, as she ground into his thick shaft.

He lined up at her wet entrance, then pushed into her with a groan. Her walls clenched around him like a fucking vice. She cried out, her nails scratching at the wall as he buried himself, her ass slamming against his hips.

The rhythm was filthy and relentless, and the sound of skin slapping against skin echoed through the tiny room. He fucked her hard, as her hips arched back into him. Her moans became desperate, broken whimpers.

"Fuck, you feel so good. You've gotten better at this," she panted, her voice trembling with every thrust.

"It's been over ten years. I've learned a few things," he said proudly, then stopped to turn her to face him.

His voice was a low growl, dripping with domination, as he pinned her against the cold, unforgiving bathroom counter. "I want you to be facing me when you cum," he snarled, his breath hot and ragged against her neck, "so you will remember exactly who fucked you into oblivion." His words weren't a request. They were a command, thick with the promise of raw, unrelenting pleasure, followed by him physically picking her up and moving her into position on the edge of the sink.

Her ass hit the counter with a sharp thunk as he shoved her legs apart like she was his property. Her thighs trembled, already slick with the mess he'd made of her, her arousal pooling shamelessly between her legs.

He guided his cock to her soaked entrance. The tip of him pressed against her, thick and throbbing, and she whimpered, her hips bucking instinctively, asking for him to enter.

He smirked and leaned close, his lips brushing her ear. "Begging already?" he taunted, his voice a filthy purr.

At her nod, he plunged in, hard and unforgiving, his cock wrecking her with each brutal thrust. She screamed; her legs locked at the knees with her pants at her ankles. Her nails clawed at his shoulders as he buried himself over and over.

She was so fucking tight it was almost suffocating, and he groaned, low and guttural, his hips pistoning into her with a rhythm that left her gasping for air.

"That's it," he growled, his hands grabbed her ass, lifting her hips to meet his every thrust. "Take it. Take all of me."

Her body was trembling, convulsing around him as he rammed with relentless precision. They might not have tomorrow, but he was going to make sure tonight would never be forgotten. He could feel her pleasure building.

"Look at me," he commanded, his voice rough and demanding. She obeyed, her eyes locking onto his as he fucked her harder and deeper. "You're not coming until I say so, understand?"

She nodded, her breath hitching as he slammed into her. His cock was his weapon of choice for the night, and from her gasps, she was loving every second of it. She might be in charge on the mission, but right now... he was.

"Good girl," he purred, his hand sliding to grip her breast, while he held her gaze. "Now cum for me."

And just like that, she shattered, she clenched around him like a vice as her orgasm ripped through her raw and fucking electric. He didn't stop, didn't slow, just kept fucking her through it, his erection dragging against her quivering walls until she was screaming his name, her body limp and trembling in his arms.

Only then did he let go, his hips stuttering as he buried himself deep one last time, his cum pulsing into her in hot, thick spurts, claiming her, marking her as his own.

This would be the incentive he needed to get himself through tomorrow. Knowing that he would do this to her every chance he could, and from the looks on her face, she would happily let him.

She clung to him, as she quietly purred in his ear, "Damn, that was so much better than I had hoped."

"I missed you," he said, setting her down on the counter and kissing her forehead.

At that, she began cleaning herself up and pulling up her pants. "There is a solid possibility of dying tomorrow. I didn't want to die with this between us," she clarified.

"Well... I think I know a better answer to your question," he said, giving a lopsided grin.

"If we make it out, what do you want to do?" she asked.

"This. This over and over again. Though I can think of a few other things I would like to add to that."

His words brought a smile to her face.

"I guess we will need to make it out of there then," she purred, pawing at his chest, as he finished buttoning his pants.

As they walked back to the safehouse, his mind imagined all the things he would do to pleasure her if they survived. They had only a few hours before they needed to get into place for their heist.

The street was empty and unnaturally silent, countering the chaos he knew was coming.

The frustration he felt toward Lydia was gone, replaced by hope... a hope for a future with Angel.

CHAPTER 9 –
THE MISSION

The first step into the access shaft was the worst. Avoiding the procession of slaves passing by had been unplanned and far more chaotic than expected. They shuffled past in silence, collars cinched tight to the chains linking them together. From the servants' whispers, Will knew this was the Order's monthly training night. Most of the slaves they saw would be casualties of the hedonistic training sessions.

The panel above them on the shaft waited, a rectangular slice of darkness cut high into the laundry sublevel of the Citadel. When Kell eased it open, it swung silently on greased hinges and released a draft that smelled of mold, rust, and old blood.

Kell wriggled through first, bracing the toe of his boot on Dorna's shoulder before disappearing into the dark.

Dorna was next. She muttered curses under her breath as she forced her way inside, and the ductwork complained with a metallic groan.

Angel went next. Her lithe body slid easily into the space.

Then it was Will's turn, and the air felt thinner.

He closed his eyes. He grew up in Media, where religion was equated with magic and banned. He had no god to pray to, so he prayed to all he knew of, hoping one might listen. He also prayed that Lydia would hold her part in the Citadel. If she failed, they would die.

With the sounds of someone coming, Will entered the tunnel and closed the grate. His boots scraped metal, his face pressed inches from the panel as he angled his torso and shimmied forward. The shaft was barely wide enough for a full-grown man, and Will's shoulders ground the walls with a rhythmic, hollow clang that threatened to vibrate every sensor for a hundred meters. But he kept moving, because the only thing worse than going forward was backing up and facing what waited behind.

He couldn't see much in the dark of the tube, as the others were much farther ahead and the tunnel was lit only by the green glow from the crystals on a necklace Angel provided.

He heard Kell announce, "Wards clear. Mechanical triggers next. There's a sensor up ahead, so be silent until I get it disarmed." His voice sounded thin and metallic, echoing through the long tube.

After a short pause, he continued, "Sensor's blinded. We're good."

The process repeated in cycles, a tense rhythm of danger and relief. Angel stayed close. When he felt the old panic rising, he only needed to glance up to see she was there, even if it was only a foot in the dark passages.

By the third junction, he had finally caught up to the rest of the group. Will's neck was kinked so hard he could barely swallow. His shirt glued to his back with sweat, the stench of laundry chemicals now fighting with a reek that made him fight the urge to gag.

One benefit of catching up was that his view improved. Angel was close enough that he couldn't avoid watching the slow shift of her hips through the tunnel. He tried not to stare, but there was nowhere else to look, and the view was very nice.

He cleared his throat. "If I have to be miserable in this confined space, at least I have a nice view. I am thinking of so many ways I will reward myself when we get out of this," he said, in a whispered tone only she could hear.

Angel replied with a measured silence, then "accidentally" lost her footing. Her heel caught his cheekbone, grinding it against the rough material with the precision of a dental drill.

Will stifled a yelp.

"Oomph. Sorry. Karma's a bitch," Angel whispered, already moving forward, her weight compact and efficient.

They pressed on. The shaft angled upward, then right, then tightened around them. Dorna's heavy breathing filled the tunnel, a dull counter beat to the steady tick of Kell's tools.

Kell stopped their progress again. "Trap ahead. Stay still."

Will froze, every muscle locked. Something ahead sizzled, then a small pop, followed by Kell's quiet sigh of relief. Will finally exhaled.

"Will. Don't panic. The shaft gets tighter here, then opens again. Breath. It will pass." Angel's voice stayed calm and soothing.

He pushed forward and could barely squeeze past. His panic built as the duct pinched his chest. His lungs refused to inflate, the air thinning into something sharp and insufficient. He tried to count heartbeats and recall Angel's breathing exercises from years ago, but his panic made the memory slip away.

Will's mouth went dry. He felt his vision gray out at the edges.

Before his vision fully collapsed into black, Angel's voice cut through the panic, low and careful. "Keep breathing, pretty boy, or I'll have to drag your corpse the rest of the way."

The absurd image of Angel hauling his dead weight through the ducts loosened the panic enough for him to breathe.

He focused on that, on her voice, and on the ridiculous notion. He dug his elbow into the seam, pulled forward, and scooted his body to keep going.

Movement flickered ahead. A rope dangled. Angel's voice echoed through the metal. "Grab the rope. We'll pull. Might make this easier."

It took all his effort to get his arms out in front of him and grab the rope. Slowly, he felt his body move through the neck of the tube. Welds in the metal walls of the shaft bit through his clothes and set his shoulder ablaze with small slices.

The world closed to a single, shivering tunnel and the promise of freedom at the other end.

He reached a wider crossbeam and nearly sobbed with relief. For a moment, he lay still, chest heaving, eyes shut.

Angel lowered her leg, not to kick him but to ground him. "You did it," she murmured, then nudged him forward. The order was clear: keep going.

The shaft turned left, and the others stopped.

"We're in position. Now we wait for the bells and hope that your girlfriend did her part," Angel relayed to him.

He noticed that the word 'girlfriend' was sharply enunciated. Surely, she must have known after last night that the relationship was over. He had planned to say something to her, but Lydia didn't get back to the room until shortly before it was time to leave. There hadn't been time.

They waited, listening carefully. When footsteps passed, they held their breath. Will's hands cramped. His mind conjured absurd images of flashing floodlights. He imagined Dorna's boot punching clean through the vent and flattening someone's skull.

He realized, with a savage kind of glee, that the Order had probably never considered that anyone would breach through these tunnels with all the wards and technical security. It was ridiculous even to him, and he was one of the people breaching this way. The real security was in the halls, though.

The bells deep in the Citadel began to chime, the sound rising through the stone in measured, deliberate tolls.

One. Two. Three. Four.

At the sixth bell, a ripple rolled through the shaft. The wards dropped. The pulse left a bitter taste on his tongue and raised every hair on his arms.

He glanced up at Angel, who had started to move.

Will braced himself, knees curled against the vent, waiting for the second when everything would finally and irrevocably fall apart.

He crawled out of the vent and froze when he saw the first dead guard lying at Dorna's feet. Kell was already pulling uniforms from his bag. They suited up and prepared for the next challenge. The lasers in the hall were down, but they knew guards and traps waited on the way to the vault.

Kell was already kneeling beside the fallen guards, rifling their pockets and checking for alarms, keys, or encoded tablets. "Nothing useful," he muttered. "These bastards travel light."

The corridor was even colder than the shaft, and his sweat steamed in the dry air. For a heartbeat, the hallway was empty, lined with statues and half-melted sconces.

Angel took the lead in her High Luminary Priestess robes, the kind that commanded automatic obedience from most Disciples.

They walked with confidence, though it was doubtful any guard expected to see two Votaries and two High Priestesses on this floor. Time was not their ally.

The first two guards appeared like a matched set. Their white robes were crisp, their boots gleaming. Will recognized the Order's elite by their gait: rigid, measured, hands never far from their sidearms. Two against four was still going to be a tough fight if it came to that.

Angel signaled a halt with a flick of her wrist. The team followed protocol and stood aside in silent deference to the elite guards.

But the Order guards knew they didn't belong on that floor. One drew his blade. "Contact. Intruders. West wall." His voice was barely above a whisper, yet it bounced off the stone like a gunshot.

Dorna stepped out, grabbed the first guard by the wrist, twisted, and hammered his skull into the marble. The sudden move caught them off guard. The impact cracked both his skull and the floor. Dorna was stronger than he gave her credit for.

The second guard reached for the comm bead, but Will was faster. He lunged, blade flashing. A single practiced cut opened the guard's throat, and blood misted across tiles and robes. They dragged the bodies into an alcove and hoped no one would notice too quickly. It had been too easy. Maybe the gods were on their side instead of Tamris.

Kell scanned ahead. "Clear. Go."

Instead of continuing their measured walk, they switched to a run. That was when they encountered six more Order guards. These were heavier, armored beneath the robes, each holding a sword in one hand and a mag pistol in the other.

"Shit," Kell hissed as he dropped behind a column just as the first shots rang out.

Dorna stepped forward with Angel flanking her. Will and Kell split left, working the perimeter.

The guards pressed forward with relentless fire.

The second guard reached for the comm bead, but Will was faster. He lunged, his blade flashing. A single practiced cut opened the man's throat, and blood misted across tile and robes. They dragged the bodies into an alcove and hoped no one would notice too quickly. Kell scanned ahead. "Clear. Go."

"Shit," Kell hissed, dropping behind a column as the first shots rang out.

Dorna stepped forward, flanked by Angel. Will and Kell split left, working the perimeter.

The guards continued their assault.

Will felt the impact before he heard it, as a slug passed so close to his skull it sheared off a lock of hair. He dove behind a pedestal, rolled, and popped up on the other side, driving a knife into the shooter's eye socket with practiced, predatory efficiency.

He glanced over just as a bullet grazed Dorna's shoulder. The round punched through her uniform, but she kept moving, her momentum unstoppable. She barreled into the guard ahead of her, lifted him by the throat, and slammed him against the balustrade. The guard's spine bent backward at a horrible angle. He stopped moving, but the attack left her exposed in the center of their formation, where she immediately dropped into hand-to-hand combat with two others.

With her deep knowledge of pressure points, Angel moved with precision, ducking low and driving her knuckles into the back of the nearest guard's knee. She called it the peroneal strike. The man's leg buckled. She followed with a throat strike, sinking her fingers into flesh and ripping it free. As he dropped, she snatched his gun. She could easily be mistaken for a priestess, but only because of her lethality.

Will turned to fire at the second guard closing on Angel, but Kell sprinted across open ground first, blades glinting. He hit the guard at full speed, ramming a knife up beneath his sternum. The guard's scream was short and wet, harmonizing with the gurgle of blood from the one with Dorna's dagger buried in his chest.

The last guard, likely their leader, had engaged Angel, and he was doing well. Maybe even winning. He moved with the precision of a lifelong duelist, his blade a silver blur, driving Angel onto the defensive. Sweat beaded on his shaved scalp, and the Order tattoos along his temples pulsed blue beneath his skin. Angel's face betrayed the first hint of strain. Tightness crept around her eyes, and her breath hitched as she twisted away from a thrust that barely missed her ribs. For the first time since he'd known her, she faced someone who matched her skill and speed.

He risked a shot, but the angle was wrong. He cursed and scanned for an opening amid the bodies. He wouldn't risk hitting her. The Order guard pressed hard, forcing Angel back against the wall. He pivoted, blade held in a perfect triangle as he drove in again. Angel barely dodged. The blade missed her cheekbone by a hair. She jabbed at his knee, one of her signature strikes, but the guard had already shifted his stance. He countered with a downward cut that would have taken her arm off at the elbow if she hadn't bent back at the last second.

Her mouth set in a grim line, eyes cold and unfocused, as if she were retreating to a place where pain and panic couldn't reach. Will could now see that Angel was losing... and losing badly.

Panic gnawed at him. Some naive part of him had always believed Angel was indestructible, that she could out-fight anyone anywhere so long as she had something to prove. But here, against this white-robed fanatic, she was outmatched. A brutal strike to the chest knocked her to the ground.

Will ran to join, snatching up a fallen short sword. The metal was cold and heavy, but it felt right in his hand. He sprinted forward and swung, aiming for the tendon behind the guard's knee.

The sword connected. The guard howled, the sound equal parts rage and surprise, but he stood his ground. Will parried and thrust, buying Angel a second to regroup.

Neither he nor the Votary expected Angel to launch herself at him with a flying kick to the chest. They slammed into the wall, and her left hand flashed to seize the guard's wrist.

The guard let her, his smile thin and bloodless.

Angel answered with a grunt of pure effort. She twisted, trying to bring her knife to his throat, but he caught her wrist and slammed it into the marble. Angel let the knife drop and, in the same motion, drove her knee into his groin. He barely reacted.

Will swung, but the man caught the blade in his bare hand, blood running down his arm. The guard whispered something in a language Will didn't recognize.

Will's strike did nothing. If the disciple felt pain, he didn't show it. Blood poured from his damaged leg, but he still stood firm. He slammed her into the wall, one hand crushing her throat while the blade dug in just below it. Her face went red, and her veins bulged in her neck. If Will moved now, he'd kill her along with the guard.

Angel exploded with strikes and punches targeting the area behind his ears, his temples, the area between his jaw and ear, then the side of his neck. He released her, gasping, and they tumbled to the floor.

Will scrambled toward them, sword ready, but the guard was already rolling to a crouch. Blood poured from the ruined leg, yet his eyes were still bright. He came at Will low and fast, blade slashing in a blur.

How was he still standing with the leg wound?

Will barely parried the thrust. He ducked a horizontal slash, hearing the blade whistle above his scalp.

The guard was toying with him, even while dying. It had to be magic. No normal man should still be standing. It was as if he wanted to kill Will slowly, to prove something, maybe to Angel. He feigned a high stab, then cut low. Will's foot slipped in a slick of blood, and he nearly went down.

Out of the corner of his eye, he saw Angel, not down, but poised and waiting. The guard saw her, too, and shifted just enough to track her. That was the opening.

Will shifted left and, as the guard moved to parry, kicked the injured leg. The guard's stance broke. Angel dove in. She wrapped her arm around his neck and twisted with all her strength. Cartilage tore, windpipe snapped, and the sound carried the unmistakable end of a life.

The guard collapsed in Angel's arms, twitched once, and went limp.

For a second, no one moved.

Angel lowered the body with a strange tenderness, as if apologizing to an old friend. He had been her most worthy opponent so far. Will just hoped there weren't more like him ahead. She stood and wiped her mouth with the back of her hand. Blood dripped from a cut above her brow, her shirt already soaked at the ribs.

Will's hands shook. The sword slipped from his grip and clattered against the marble. They were alive. She was alive. A feeling of awe hit him, and he pulled her into his arms, kissing the top of her head.

"I need to remember not to make you mad," Will said, wiping blood spatter from his face with one finger before releasing her and scanning for the others.

Will's heart pounded. Kell crouched beside Dorna as she grunted and popped her dislocated shoulder back into place with a wince. She wiped blood from her arm and stood, walking toward Angel.

Six bodies lay strewn across the room, mortal wounds keeping them down and the light gone from their eyes. But his team stood.

"Nice," Dorna said as she surveyed the scene.

Will looked to Angel, already collecting and reloading the guard's pistol, eyes scanning for more. "We're behind schedule," she said. "Move."

Kell wiped his blade clean on a dead man's cloak, then signaled the all-clear. They ran, and Will's thoughts broke free with brutal clarity.

Lydia.

She had completed her task, clearly, but he wondered if she had gotten away. She was supposed to create a distraction to pull the elite guards away from the vault. Will pictured her, wild red hair and bright smile, flammable as ever. If she hadn't made it out after placing the items, everything ahead would be harder. He pushed the worry aside. They needed to focus on the task at hand.

They stopped when the hall narrowed and the tiles changed. According to the plans, there was an obstacle here. The walls were crowded with relics and glyphs, every surface polished to a blinding sheen.

Kell slowed and lifted a hand. "If Will's interrogation was accurate, once we get past this section, there should be fewer guards... assuming we make it past," he whispered.

The trap was almost insultingly obvious: raised tiles, just a shade off-color from the rest, hiding pressure plates beneath. Will watched as Kell picked his way across, toes probing, weight never fully committed. He motioned for Will to follow his exact path.

Will did, mimicking every footfall. Halfway across, he lost his balance and rocked forward. He felt the click under his boot.

Kell froze. Will's pulse stopped cold. He shifted his weight back, praying the plate would reset.

It didn't. A hiss sounded above them.

"Down!" Kell shouted.

A storm of tiny needles shot from the ceiling, thin as sewing pins. Will hit the floor and felt a dozen sharp pricks through his robe, but none broke through to his skin.

"There has got to be a disarming mechanism somewhere," Angel spat. "Find it!"

With him frozen in place, Kell found a small switch and pressed it.

"Try it now," he offered.

Cautiously, Will pressed the same plate with his robe covering his boot. No movement. Safe. The rest followed through and joined Kell at the switch.

Another thirty steps brought them to a turn, and at the far end, the tiles changed again. This time, the threat was obvious. Three swinging blades swept through slits in the wall like pendulums. Ancient, but still razor sharp. Angel waited, counted the cycles, and made her move between sweeps.

"The blades arced down every fifteen seconds. Just enough room for someone my size to slip through. I'll go." She didn't wait for approval. She slipped past the first blade, turning sideways as metal sliced the air inches from her skin.

He held his breath as she waited to make the next move. She crossed at the perfect second, but when the next blade swept past, a strip of fabric tore free and spun into the air. Will gasped.

"It's just my sleeve. I'm fine," she said.

She waited, then stepped past the final blade. She scanned the wall, found another switch, and flipped it. The blades froze mid-swing.

Kell grinned, a rare flash of joy. "Told you she was the best," he said to Will.

"Don't I know," Will said, smiling.

Once everyone crossed, Kell rearmed the mechanism. The whoosh of blades filled the hall again. They continued forward until the tiles changed again.

The final obstacle was a glyph set into the floor: a spiral of runes etched into obsidian stone, glowing with an eerie blue-green luminescence that cast sickly shadows across their faces.

Kell crouched at its edge, sweat beading on his forehead, lips pursed into a thin white line. "From the schematics, I couldn't tell if it's motion or weight-activated?"

"It's motion. The first challenge was weight," Angel said, her breath warm against Will's neck as she leaned over his shoulder.

Will's throat went dry as Kell unfurled a packet of fine silver powder that caught the dim light like crushed stars. With surgeon-steady hands, he sprinkled it over the glyph. The powder hissed faintly as it settled into the grooves, dulling the phosphorescent shine to a sullen glow.

"Okay. That should blind the sensor long enough for me to cross."

Will's heart hammered against his ribs as Kell stepped onto the edge of the spiral, each footfall was deliberate and precise. The runes pulsed beneath him, in perfect synchronization with Kell's heartbeat. When he reached the other side, his fingers danced across the switch. The glyph dimmed further but didn't go out entirely. He exhaled, relief sharp and short. Three obstacles down.

"Be careful where you step," Kell warned, voice tight. "It may be disarmed, but it's still dangerous. Move clockwise only."

The hallway opened into a grand antechamber at the far end, massive and carved with ancient script. Silent stone sentinels flanked the entrance, empty-eyed yet watchful.

Will took a breath, felt the sweat cool on his forehead. His muscles trembled with adrenaline. He glanced back. Angel met his gaze, equal parts steel and empathy. The cut on her forehead had stopped bleeding, and at some point she had smeared ointment across it.

"Almost there," she whispered.

The vault doors dominated the corridor. Even from here, Will could feel their weight and the magic protecting them. The air thickened, and an electric tingle crawled over his skin. Each panel was carved from black stone, inlaid with veins of living crystal that shimmered with each pulse like the Citadel's heart. Two more stone sentinels guarded the threshold. Empty-eyed, yet somehow aware, runes spiraling up their legs and into their massive shoulders.

Kell didn't hesitate. He approached the seam, pulled his tools, and set to work on the final ward. It was a knot of shifting glyphs that crawled in and out of reality, never sitting still long enough to read. Will's eyes watered just trying to look at it.

Angel fanned out, covering the right flank, pistol drawn and steady. Dorna placed herself between Kell and the statues, ready to protect him at all costs.

Will stood near Kell, watching him and the ends of the hall. In the distance, the alarm klaxons started to whine with a sour, almost organic sound, like a bone flute. Backup systems were cycling. They had minutes, maybe less, before the Citadel reached full alert. At least the EMP would keep the laser grid down.

Kell's hands moved with a speed Will envied. On the first attempt, a tendril of magic sliced across his knuckles, drawing thin lines of blood. The second attempt was no better. He muttered a mix of curses and half-formed prayers, fingers dancing over the swirling glyphs. At every touch, the runes shifted. Sometimes they receded. Sometimes they lashed out with blue fire. The static in the air thickened, lifting the hairs on Will's arms and coating his tongue with iron.

"It's changing too quickly," Kell said, voice tight. "Two more attempts before the system locks us out." The glyphs flashed, bright and violent. He screamed. The sound was raw and high, edged with panic. The tendril carved a deep spiral into his flesh, blood welling up instantly. Dorna lunged, trying to swat the magic away, but the ward recoiled and vanished back into the seam.

Kell dropped to his knees, clutching his arm. "I'm good, I'm good. Just give me a second." His face had gone pale, his lips trembling, but he still pulled a new tool from his vest and set to work with his left hand.

Angel's voice was ice. "You have thirty seconds, Kell."

Footsteps echoed from the corridor behind, a percussive march of discipline and hatred. When the whoosh of the blades fell silent, they all knew time was almost gone.

Kell's last tool was a needle of blue glass that penetrated the very center of the glyph spiral. With a hiss and a rush of displaced air, the ward collapsed inward, sucking the light and flame with it. The last flick of magic still caught Kell's hand, leaving a deep, burning slice. The doors groaned, then cracked open on a seam of utter blackness.

Will and Dorna caught Kell as he slumped sideways and dragged him through the gap. Angel brought up the rear, firing a warning shot down the corridor to slow the first wave of heavy boots pounding down the hall. Before he passed the control panel, Kell smashed the keypad with the hilt of his knife.

When they stepped inside, the vault felt like another world. As the doors sealed shut, clicks and heavy thuds echoed through the room. They wasted no time. Kell and Dorna shoved a nearby shelf over with a thundering crash, barring the door. It would slow the guards. It could also entomb them if there was no second exit. They had to prioritize looking for another exit, as well as the Tomes.

With the entrance secured, Will turned and finally took in the vault. It was massive, larger than the athletic field at his high school in Media. The darkness swallowed the far end. He couldn't see how deep the vault stretched.

A short flight of steps led down to the vault floor. The ceiling soared five stories overhead, its arches converging around a massive crystal obelisk that rose from the floor. It stood nearly as tall as the buildings in Media's City Center. Its tip met the dome ceiling above. Gold inlay along the arches caught the crystal light, revealing ancient runes etched into every curve.

Shelves the size of city walls created a maze within the space, each packed with grimoires, jars, and relics that whispered with dormant power.

At the bottom of the stairs, a long table sat, waiting, with a massive book open on its stand. Two paths split left and right behind it. There was no clear sign of where the Tomes might be hidden. Angel motioned toward the book.

The air shimmered around them, thick with compressed magic that hummed against Will's skin. Will's skin tingled as he moved deeper into the room, his shadow flickering and splitting in the warped light.

Could they really be this lucky?

The open pages revealed an alphabetized index. Angel flipped to T. Halfway down the page, she found it: Tomes of Moreth. A symbol and two numbers marked its location.

"That must be the shelf and the shelf location. We just need to find the shelf with this symbol," Angel said.

"Dorna and I will go left. You two take the right. Call out if you see the symbol," Kell said, wrapping his injured hand with a strip of cloth pulled from his bag.

"Don't forget to be on the lookout for another way out of here," Angel reminded.

Will holstered his blade and followed Angel, the world telescoping to the task at hand, as Dorna and Kell headed off in the other direction.

Before disappearing into the maze of shelves, Will glanced back. White robes flashed at the vault entrance. The Order was already there, pounding on the sealed doors with the force of a mob. He was honestly surprised the barrier had held this long.

CHAPTER 10 –
THE VAULT'S GUARDIAN

Will and Angel searched the shelves for their marker: a starburst crossed by a diagonal slash. Once they understood the placement system, they scanned shelf after shelf for their mark. The shelves stretched in endless aisles of relics, tomes, and forbidden curios. Many pulsed with the low hum of ancient magic and carried the weight of dust and temptation.

At shoulder height, rows of scrolls wrapped in silk or embedded in glass tubes lined the shelves. He brushed a scroll with his fingertips and felt the thrum of forbidden knowledge beneath the casing. He forced himself to move on. The next bay offered only worse distractions: a crown of gleaming opals that shivered and flickered with internal light, a short sword forged from a single perfect diamond, a mask shaped from gold wire so thin it was nearly transparent.

All of it was priceless. All of it was entirely outside the mission parameters.

Still, his hand lingered on the jeweled hilt for a heartbeat too long. Then he palmed it and slid it into an empty sheath.

He risked a glance at Angel. Of course, she had noticed. She always did. She shot him a look that said, *Focus or I will kill you myself*, then turned the next corner.

They advanced in a zigzag, pausing at every shelf to check the symbol. They pressed onward, deeper into the vault. The deeper they walked, the more opulent the hoard became. It felt obscene, even to Will. Weapons built for a single purpose and never used. Gems carved into flawless shapes only to be forgotten. Clockwork automatons still ticking inside glass prisons.

Will found himself longing for Kell's magical bag, the one that could swallow anything without complaint. He'd give his left hand for one now. Maybe both.

The vault door shuddered under a barrage of blows, each impact reverberating through the cavernous space like thunder trapped underground. Will's eyes darted to the massive steel barrier, its ancient hinges groaning in protest but holding firm. Relief washed over him at the sight of it still sealed shut, though a cold knot formed in his stomach as he realized they could not exit through the main doors blocked by an army of furious Order guards.

A shadow passed over them, followed by a metallic clatter somewhere only a few shelves away. A rush of displaced air ripped down the aisle, followed by a high-pitched shriek. Will went cold.

Angel dropped into a crouch, eyes scanning for movement. Will mirrored her, every sense sharpened. The noise echoed through the vault, impossible to pinpoint.

The shriek continued, inhuman and sharp enough to make his teeth ache. The sound belonged to something large, and every instinct screamed to avoid it. It was rage and hunger and terror, all bound into a single, piercing wail.

Will's muscles seized, but he forced himself to move. He unslung his weapon, checked the magazine, and pulled a knife into his other hand. He nodded at Angel, signaling readiness. She nodded back and gestured for a slow, careful advance.

They moved as one, shelf by shelf, toward the source of the noise. His body tried to slow him at every step.

Will stayed close to the shelves as he advanced. Angel was two steps ahead when the shriek finally shifted into a low, guttural snarl. At the next junction, she paused, crouched, and peered around the shelf. Her eyes widened, only a flicker.

He risked a glance.

Fuck.

A scaled creature towered nearly twenty feet tall, wings folded tight to its body. He had never seen a dragon this close, but he knew exactly what he was looking at. Not full-grown, but already the height of three men. Its scales shone deep red. It prowled the aisle ahead. Its claws gripped the shelving with surgical precision, leaving gouges in ancient hardwood with every shift of weight. A heavy chain wrapped one hind leg, the links thick as a man's wrist, leading back to the crystal obelisk in the vault's center. A light blinked on the device. He could only imagine what it was for.

The beast moved with the deadly intent of something born to hunt. It stalked along the tops of the shelves, tongue flicking, nostrils flaring as it tasted the air. The effect was both majestic and obscene. Its body was lithe muscle and sinuous grace, but its eyes glittered with hunger and bitter intelligence.

Will pressed himself into the shadows. Angel inched back until their faces were only centimeters apart. Her breath stayed steady, but her hands trembled by the slightest fraction. She whispered, "We can't get past that thing. We wait for it to move."

He nodded. Patience was the only option. If it caught their scent, they were doomed. All they could do was hope it was hunting something else.

Then, from across the vault, Kell's voice rang out in triumph.

"We've found them! Tomes secured in my bag."

Will's heart stopped. They risked a glance around the corner to gauge the creature's reaction. The dragon's head whipped around toward Kell's voice. It flexed its wings and launched from its perch. The air blast alone knocked Will and Angel back against the shelves.

They ran, instinct overriding everything, sprinting through labyrinthine aisles toward Kell. The shelves blurred past. Will risked one glance to the side. He could see nothing through the shelves, but he heard it land, the chain dragging in a lethal arc behind it.

He rounded a corner at full speed and stopped short. Kell stood at the far end of a long aisle, calling Dorna, who was still studying a shelf. Kell held his knife, drawn toward the beast.

"Get down!" Will screamed, too late.

The wyrmling pounced, claws outstretched like daggers of polished obsidian. It landed with a thunderous impact, shaking the shelves and sending ancient artifacts rattling against each other. Not three feet from Kell, its pupils narrowed to vertical slits, focusing with predatory precision. The serrated ivory knives, the beast called teeth, filled its jaws. They snapped like the sound of a steel trap closing. One moment, Kell's terrified face was there; the next, his head was gone, torn off as cleanly as if by a guillotine. His body stood upright for one impossible second before crumpling, his arterial blood spurting in rhythmic pulses across the marble floor and nearby relics. The magical bag, its leather now slick with crimson, remained wrapped around his ruined torso, its enchantments still humming with indifferent power.

Dorna screamed. It was an animal sound, pure terror and pain. She retreated a few steps, hands shaking, then froze, face going blank. The beast let out a satisfied shriek.

She looked from Kell's body back to the creature, planted her feet, and drew her sword. Her eyes locked on the beast.

Angel pulled Will down behind the nearest row. "That device is controlling it," she said, her voice pitched low and deadly calm. "Red dragons don't do this," she hissed. "Not by nature. That device is driving it mad. It isn't in control. The EMP should have shut it down, unless the vault is shielded."

Will tracked her gaze to the mechanism affixed to the wyrmling's leg. The light on it pulsed, in time with the dragon's rage. He had no idea where she learned that lore, but she sounded sure. *Red dragons might not be killers, but this one obviously was.* He needed to help Dorna... one way or the other.

For a split second, Will saw the madness in its eyes, the pain behind it. He wondered if dragons could go mad, if this one had simply spent too long chained in the dark. He nodded, heart hammering, unable to look away from the carnage. He stood with his weapon drawn, ready to fight, even knowing how pointless it might be. The dragon's head bobbed up, bits of Kell still clinging to its maw. It shook once, twice, flinging gore across the shelves, then fixed its gaze first on him, then on Dorna.

Angel gripped Will's shoulder, her nails digging in so hard he felt blood bead beneath her touch. "We must get Kell's bag. That's the mission," she said. "No matter what." Angel continued, "You have to get it off the corpse. I'll go for the controller."

Will nodded. He felt numb as he watched the wyrmling lower its head and prepare to strike.

The dragon stalked toward Dorna, recognizing her as the greater threat. With murderous intent in her eyes, Dorna met its gaze with a defiance that bordered on holy, her sword steady.

Will sprinted the distance and skidded to Kell's body. The remains were gruesome, the bag still strapped around what was left of his shoulder. He grabbed the leather, feeling it vibrate with a wild, hungry magic. The bag's energy bled into his palm and snaked up his arm, leaving a wake of cold fire along his nerves. He almost dropped it. Through sheer will, he gritted his teeth and held on.

Dorna charged again, sword raised in both hands. She screamed, a war cry that made the hair rise on Will's neck. The wyrmling ignored her until the last instant, then spat a cone of flame so hot it turned the world around them white.

Dorna never stood a chance. The fire hit her full-on, a white-hot inferno that turned her leather armor to bubbling tar against her skin. Her hair vaporized in an instant, her exposed flesh blackening and splitting like overcooked meat, revealing the charred bone beneath. The smell of burning fat and singed hair filled the air as her body crumpled, still twitching. She didn't even have time to scream before the superheated sword dropped from her skeletal fingers and clattered to the marble floor, leaving a scorch mark where it landed.

Above, he heard the crash of shelves. He looked up to see Angel scaling the racks like a spider, her fingers finding every crack and seam. The wyrmling roared as it caught sight of her and snapped at the air with its deadly jaws. Angel leapt and flipped, the chain missing her heel by less than an inch.

"Draw its attention. If it flames again, grab a shelf. The ones behind Dorna didn't ignite. They must be protected. It should shield you."

Will clutched the bag and yelled, "Hey, you ugly bastard!" It wasn't poetry, but it worked.

The beast swung its head his way, eyes burning with a hate so pure it stunned him. It inhaled, chest ballooning. Will grabbed the nearest shelf just as a sheet of red fire rolled over his head. The heat was blistering, but it didn't touch him.

Will didn't have time to appreciate Angel's brilliance. Through the smoke, he saw her only a meter from the dragon's leg, knife out, eyes locked on the device. She hacked at the chain, sparks flashing as the metal screamed. She switched tactics, reaching directly for the glowing light.

The wyrmling sensed her and pivoted, slamming a claw into the shelving where she stood. The shelf shuddered but held. Angel braced, then launched herself at the wyrmling's leg. Will tried to pull the creature's attention again, yelling and jumping.

Angel shifted tactics and wrapped both arms around the dragon's leg as her knife plunged into the device. The dragon howled, thrashing and twisting, slamming its body against the shelves in a desperate bid to dislodge her. Its tail hit him, knocking him back.

Will staggered to his feet, wrapping the bag around his chest, and ran straight into the chaos. He reached the bottom of the shelf; his eyes locked on Angel's desperate struggle to rip the device free.

He knew in that moment that nothing in the world would ever be easy with Angel. She fought to free the wyrmling from its torment, and he knew he'd never be able to forget this moment. Instead of plunging her knives into its chest or firing her weapon, she was trying to save it while it tried to kill her.

She was a better person than he was, in so many ways.

He couldn't let her be harmed. He scrambled higher, using knotholes and edges as handholds.

The dragon's head followed him, jaw opening and closing with a thunderous snap. It tried to bite, but the shelf's wards repelled even those diamond teeth. Will reached the top row and ran along the edge. Soon, he was level with the wyrmling's face, only meters away.

He pulled out the stolen short sword and raised it. He could feel an arcane energy pulsing from it, but he didn't know what it would do. He planned to wait for the weapon to respond, then leap off the shelf and hang on the supports if the flames came. At the first snap, everything slowed. The wyrmling moved as if underwater, giving him time to shift out of range.

At the dragon's ankle, Angel worked furiously. From a distance, it looked as though her fingers had bloodied as she tore at the mechanism. The dragon froze mid-breath, shuddered, and twisted, trying to shake her loose. Then it realized the chain was no longer attached. She clung with her legs and one arm while the other chipped at the device.

"Almost there!" she yelled.

Will knew the distraction wouldn't last. The dragon opened its jaws, ready to roast him again.

Will jumped and twisted, grabbing the shelf with one hand before the flames hit. His hand landed on a ceramic orb etched with glyphs of cold. He hurled it. When it hit the dragon's maw, the magic detonated in a burst of frost that glazed the wyrmling's face, freezing its nostrils and jawline. It recoiled, roaring in surprise.

Angel seized the moment. With a strained scream, she wrenched the device free from the wyrmling's leg. The mechanism popped, spraying sparks and a gout of blue flame. Angel held on, then dropped to the ground with the broken device clenched in her fist.

The wyrmling froze. Its eyes widened, the fury draining away until only a bright, wary intelligence remained. The creature trembled, every muscle shivering in a wave down its spine. It looked around, saw Angel, then the shattered controller. Relief flickered across its face.

For a moment, no one moved.

The wyrmling lowered its head, touching its snout to the ground in front of Angel. When it finally spoke, its voice sounded like a landslide wrapped in velvet, young and scared.

"Free. I am free. It hurt so bad. I want to go home. I want my family."

Will stared, not daring to breathe at hearing the voice. He had never heard a dragon speak. Angel stepped forward, never breaking eye contact with the creature, and knelt at the wyrmling's side.

"We'll help you," she said. "But we need to leave. Can you help us get out?"

The wyrmling nodded, looking up at the high ceiling, the locked doors, the world beyond. "I can, but I'm not strong enough to break the walls or carry you." Its voice sounded exhausted and broken.

Will felt something shift in the air. The hatred was gone, replaced by desperate yearning. He felt a new respect for the impossible balance of violence and mercy Angel carried in her veins. He would have planned to kill the creature. She saw beyond that.

He climbed back up the shelves to stand beside her.

They had the treasure, the lives of the city, and a dragon in their debt. They just needed to get out alive.

For the first time since entering the Citadel, Will let himself believe they might live through this, then immediately hated himself for the thought. His gaze dropped to the scorched ground where they lost Dorna, her final scream still echoing in his ears, and to the pool of blood congealing around Kell's body. Hope and despair warred within him. Their survival suddenly seemed possible, yet it came at a price he wasn't sure he could justify.

Up close, the wyrmling was all teeth and terror, but Will saw the quiver in its legs and the way it shrank from Angel's hand as she reached toward its bloody maw.

"I'm sorry they did this to you. I bet you were just a hatchling when they stole you. I once traveled to the Eastern

Draco Mountains near Gosual and met a Red dragon family there. They were kind to me and helped me escape terrible men. I learned then how extraordinary dragons are. What they did to you is horrible. To starve and traumatize a youngling and force you to kill is evil."

The creature leaned into her hand as she rested it against the dragon's brow. Will couldn't stop a faint smile. Angel was better than he would ever be. He could only hope to be worthy of her one day.

Will opened the magical bag, Kell's last legacy, still damp with the man's blood, and visualized what he needed. The explosives. It responded, revealing an assortment of items, but explosives weren't his expertise. Nothing resembled the detonators he knew or the ones he had seen Dorna use.

His hand closed around a heavy, greasy cylinder he recognized as one of Dorna's charges. He tried thinking of a detonator, but nothing appeared. Kell was smart. He would have known it would be better to keep them separate, and who would he trust more than Dorna?

He thought fast, scanning the wreckage and the dragon's battered body. "I have explosives that can get us through the ceiling wall," he said. "But I'll need your fire to set them off. We will use what is left of your chain and the rope to climb down. Can you help with that?"

The wyrmling nodded, eyes brightening. "Yes," it said. "Yes. Want to go home."

Will looked at Angel, who grinned and shrugged. "I knew you would be useful," she said with a smirk, still stroking the massive creature's bloody head.

Just then, the ground shook with muffled explosions outside the vault.

"Dorna's charges must be going off. That should give us cover," he said as he climbed, knives in hand, scaling the shelves and then the smooth marble dome, using the blades like climbing cams, stabbing them into the cracks. With pounding still hammering at the vault door, Will moved with the urgency of someone who knew every second could be his last.

At the top, he found a seam, likely an old maintenance hatch, sealed by centuries of arrogance. He wedged the charge above the hatch and scrambled down, leaving a rope of twine and silk trailing behind.

At the bottom, the dragon waited, tail curled like a cat's, eyes fixed on the ceiling. When they had taken appropriate cover, Will signaled, and the wyrmling gathered itself, flexed its wings, and leapt. The chain on its leg snapped taut, holding it just beneath the dome. It looked down at Will and Angel, then up, and unleashed a single, narrow stream of fire.

The flame hit the charge, and for a moment, there was only silence.

Then the world exploded. The ceiling disintegrated with a deafening crack that reverberated through Will's bones and set his teeth vibrating. A blinding white-hot flash seared his vision, leaving purple afterimages dancing across his eyes. Massive chunks of ancient marble and granite crashed down around them, pulverizing into deadly shrapnel upon impact. Dust billowed in choking clouds, filling his nostrils with the acrid smell of scorched stone and ancient mortar.

Will threw himself over Angel as jagged fragments rained down, slicing his exposed skin. Through watering eyes, he saw the dragon clinging to the wall, talons embedded deep in the stone, scales glittering with debris, utterly unbothered by the destruction. It swung its serpentine neck down toward them, extending a scarred, blood-red claw large enough to crush a man's skull.

"You are free now," Angel said. "You owe us nothing."

The dragon shook its head, the motion oddly human. "A debt is owed. I will remember. If you live, find me. I am Cerveny Plamen. I will go where you said and find my kin."

Angel lifted the chain, and the dragon bit down on it. She perched beside it and stroked its muzzle once before it launched into the air. They gripped the shelves to steady themselves against the rush of wind from its wings. It flew upward, squeezed through the breach in the ceiling, pulled the chain behind it, then released.

They climbed the wall of knives to the opening, the bright midday sun burning their eyes as they ascended. Then they climbed down the hanging chain to what was likely the roof of the fourth floor.

The city stretched out below them in chaos, fires raging across the landscape. The air at this height was cold and clean. One floor below, a ledge waited. They climbed down to find the next marker of their escape route.

Will watched Cerveny set several blazes along its path, then climb into the morning sky toward its home. The shriek it left behind was different this time, tinged with something that sounded almost like pleasure.

Angel brushed against him, warm and solid at his side. "We did it," she said.

"We did it," he agreed, "but we aren't safe yet." He opened the bag, checked the Tomes, and closed it again. "Let's get out of here before anything else shows up."

They climbed down the building wall, using ledges and rooflines to guide their escape. For a while, neither spoke. At the edge of the roof, Angel turned and looked out over the burning city, the sun bright overhead.

"It looks like Lydia and the boys did their part," she said, gesturing at the destruction below.

He had almost forgotten about Lydia.

"I guess we should meet her at the rendezvous point," he said, though he hoped Angel would change the plan. Surely Lydia could find safety on her own. Then he remembered he was trying to make better choices... for Angel.

"I guess so. She did her part, and she deserves to know if we made it or not." Angel smiled, though he thought he saw something wistful in her eyes.

"You know I'm telling her immediately there's no relationship waiting for her. Right?" He needed her to understand that.

"I heard you."

Will cast one last lingering glance at the shredded ceiling, mentally cataloging the treasures he had left behind, the ones he would never touch. But the bag felt good at his side.

With Angel beside him and the bag secure, he finally let himself believe in something dangerous: hope.

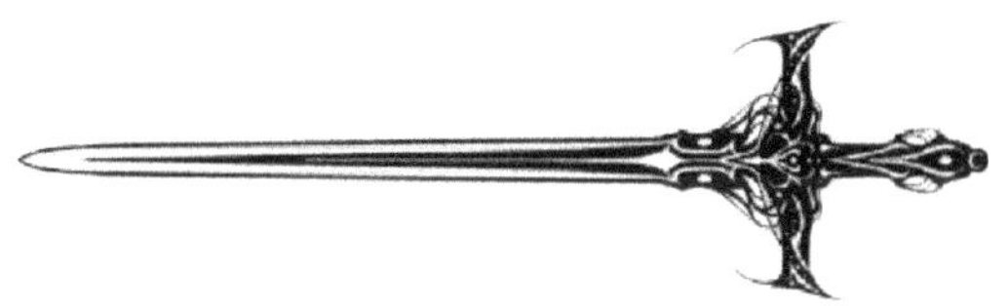

CHAPTER 11 –
GREAT LOVE AND GREAT LOSS

They ran through the city streets, keeping to the edges and away from crowds. The chill sliced through Will's battered Votary uniform, raising bumps along his skin. Angel ran beside him, still disguised as a high priestess, though her ceremonial garb was torn and streaked with soot. Her hair, usually a severe helmet, now hung ragged across her face. They were running on fumes. They hadn't eaten since morning, and exhaustion dragged at every step.

As the dragon flew away from them, the city was alive with chaos and dragon fire, and it seemed every disciple was out on the streets. Smoke from still-burning buildings hung over the skyline, mingling with the sharper scent of burnt flesh. Sirens bleated like dying lambs. He couldn't tell if they were for the fires or for them.

Angel guided them along the east wall, blending with the late-afternoon movement. They would rendezvous at the Resistance safehouse after sunset.

As they rounded a corner at the edge of a square, Angel slowed. They were near the industrial center Lydia was supposed to burn as a distraction. She stopped him with a rugged grip on his arm. "Trouble," she whispered.

Will followed her gaze, expecting another Order checkpoint, maybe a clutch of overzealous guards. Instead, he saw a massive fire. An entire housing block burned. Four stories of stone and old timber were fully engulfed. The flames licked at the sky, painting the narrow streets red and orange. Figures darted through the chaos. Some carried children. Some carried nothing but the clothes on their backs. Next to the chaos stood an untouched industrial complex.

Will froze. "No! It can't be," he said, the words flat, useless. Lydia must have been behind this. Lydia murdered hundreds of innocents. This area was nowhere near the dragon's path, and this building was next to the building Lydia was tasked to burn. It had to be her.

A woman stumbled into the gutter, her gown half-burned, a baby clutched to her chest. Her face was streaked with soot and panic. Behind her, a second-floor window burst outward, sending a rain of glass onto the street. A little boy leapt out, arms windmilling, and landed hard on the cobbles. He rolled once, twice, then lay still. An old man, likely the boy's grandfather, followed. Will watched as his body snapped on the landing. The air reeked of blood and scorched flesh.

Angel pulled Will back, her voice a quiet knife. "We can't help them. Keep walking. There are too many of the Order around."

Will couldn't leave. His mouth fell open, and no sound came out. He stood rooted, eyes fixed on the chaos. A charred toy lay in the grass. A wooden horse with one wheel missing. Broken. He picked it up. The wood was still warm.

Angel hissed, "Will. The Tomes. We must protect the Tomes."

He wanted to listen to her, but the knowledge that Lydia had done this slapped him back to reality. This was no accident, and it was an act of cruelty. One of pure malevolence.

"Lydia," he whispered.

Angel didn't answer. She didn't need to. She had come to the same conclusion.

At the far end of the street, a patrol of four Order Disciples appeared in black tabarded breastplates, visors down, each armed with a mag pistol. Their uniforms marked them as entry-level. They were heading toward the survivors until they noticed Will and Angel standing at the street's edge. There was no way either of them looked the part in their current state.

"Stop. Papers," the guard barked. The cowl and face covering distorted his voice, but the pitch revealed he was young and male. Angel stepped ahead, hands visible, and her face set in priestess serenity.

"We are on an emergency errand from the High Luminary." The guard eyed her, then shifted his gaze to Will.

"Password," he said, gesturing to the three guards flanking him. They raised their pistols in perfect choreography.

Angel replied without hesitation. "Aurora Tertius."

The leader didn't blink. "Incorrect. Final warning."

Will felt his gut drop. Angel's hand twitched. She was calculating odds, weighing options, probably wishing she could take back her last words. The guards spread out, forming a loose arc to encircle them.

Will moved before he could think. He closed the distance to the nearest guard in three long strides, ducking low. The guard's mag-pistol flashed, the shot tearing through Will's sleeve and searing the skin beneath but missing bone. He twisted the guard's wrist, felt the tiny bones snap, and wrenched the gun free.

Angel exploded into motion beside him. She closed on the second guard with a precise elbow to the neck, then a knee to the gut. The guard doubled over, retched, and dropped the pistol. Angel caught it one-handed, flipped it, and fired a point-blank shot into the guard's chest. The man crumpled as smoke curled from the fresh wound.

Will was already in the thick of it. The third guard leveled his weapon at Will's head. Will hurled the stolen mag-pistol in his face and dove. The guard stumbled. Will grabbed the man's boot, yanked him off-balance, and slammed his head against the pavement with a sickening crunch.

As the guard fell, Will looked at the last disciple, the leader, who had held back. The man steadied his gun and locked on Angel. She circled him, keeping her body between Will and the line of fire.

"Drop it," Angel ordered.

The guard smirked. "You first, bitch."

Angel didn't move. She edged forward, weapon trained on the leader's groin. "You know who I am?"

"Don't care," the leader spat. "You're dead."

The guard fired, but Angel was already rolling right, landing in a crouch before returning fire. The shot caught the leader's thigh. He screamed but stayed standing. Instead, he drew a short, curved blade as black as tar and charged.

Angel met him, side-stepping at the last second and bringing the butt of her gun down on his wrist. The blade clattered away. Angel jammed her thumb into the guard's throat, and he dropped to his knees, gasping and drooling. She shot him in the back of the head.

It was over in seconds.

Will staggered to his feet, breathing hard, arm slick with his own blood. "You, okay?"

Angel nodded, but her face was pale, and she favored her left leg. "It's not serious. Keep moving."

At the next intersection, Angel stopped and doubled over, hands on her knees.

"You good?" Will asked, but she didn't answer. Instead, she peeled back her robe and revealed a mag-pistol wound low on her chest, just below the bottom rib, spilling dark blood.

The world went quiet.

"You're hit," he said, the words dumb and obvious.

Angel nodded, a grimace twisting her mouth. "Guess I'm not as invincible as you thought."

The wound was bleeding fast. He checked her back. No exit. The bullet was still inside.

Will ripped the sleeve from his already ruined shirt, folded it into a crude pad, and pressed it against the wound. Angel hissed but didn't flinch. Her blood was shockingly dark, and it soaked the makeshift dressing in seconds.

"We need a doctor," he said.

"No time," she replied, voice thin. "We need to get to the safehouse. I can make it."

At first, she tried to lean on him, but he lifted her into his arms and ran. Each step left a trail of blood they couldn't afford, but Will kept going. His only thought was getting her to the safe house. Running while keeping pressure on the wound was agony, but he forced himself on. She was fading fast, her skin growing paler and her breathing slowing.

It should have been him. She was the better person. She deserved to live.

Maybe cauterization would work once they reached safety, though the thought of the pain it would cause her turned his stomach. Then a voice called out from his left, hoarse but familiar.

"Hawk! Is that you?"

Will turned and recognized Chase, the Resistance guard from the stables. Chase fell into stride beside him, with Connelly close behind.

Both wore civilian jackets over scavenged armor as they ran alongside him.

"Status?" Chase asked, eyes flicking to Angel in Will's arms.

"Hit, liver wound. No exit wound in the back, so the bullet is still inside," Will said, voice flat. "We need to get her to the safehouse to stop the bleeding."

"Stop now," Connelly said as he pulled a vial from his coat and uncapped it. "This will help temporarily."

At the presentation, Will stopped and lowered Angel onto a patch of soft earth beside the street.

Chase ripped open her top without hesitation, exposing the wound and her breast bindings, and poured the contents directly over it. The liquid fizzed like battery acid. Angel woke with a full-throated scream, then clamped her teeth and shuddered, grabbing onto Will's wrist. Will's heart broke at her pain.

Chase watched, unflinching. "We still need the bullet out, but that should stop the bleeding until we can get her help. The crew is meeting at the river bridge extraction point."

Will nodded, unable to trust his voice. He watched the bleeding slow and stop. Angel opened one eye, found his, and managed a weak smile. "Mind covering my chest?" she rasped. She made a failed attempt to lift her arms.

A crash echoed from the next street as a patrol kicked in a door. Shouts followed. An Order patrol. Too close.

"Fuck," Will hissed. "They'll follow us now."

Connelly wiped his hands, stood, and met Will's eyes. "Her only chance is reaching the extraction point."

Chase nodded. "We'll take Angel, get her to the medics, but we can't have them following us. Can you draw the hounds off, to give us cover?"

Will felt the old anger coil inside him. "I... I want to go with her." The words cracked in his throat. "Can one of you lead them away?"

Connelly shook his head. "We can't risk them catching the team and what you stole. If you want her to survive, you need to separate. Now. She's halfway gone already. You want her to die?"

His heart clenched at the thought of losing her again. After all these years of missing her, to finally find her again, to have her choose him... He had to walk away to keep her safe. If he left her, he might never see her again.

Angel's fingers touched his wrist. She looked up at him. "I don't like it either, but they're right," she breathed. "You need to deliver the Tomes to our contacts in Sarhan. If the Order reaches the extraction point, the mission dies with us."

He blinked against the burn in his eyes and nodded. "Fine. But I will find you."

Her face softened into a smile. "I'll hold you to that."

He kissed her gently, brushed her cheek, then passed her limp body into Chase's arms. The moment she was secure, Chase and Connelly took off, disappearing just as the patrol rounded the corner and spotted Will.

He bolted, drawing their attention and pulling them after him. He kept low, sprinting through a maze of back alleys and piles of refuse. A glance confirmed three figures in pursuit, two peeling off to flank him from the next street.

He was exhausted. They were good. But he was determined.

Will doubled back, vaulted a fence, and slid under a rusted trash chute into the sewer run-off. The stench was horrific, but the constant runoff masked his movement, and he climbed back onto the road after several hundred steps.

He used a length of gutter hanging from the roof to haul himself onto the roof of the next building, dropping down to the alley on the other side. He landed hard, pain flaring in his knees, but he kept moving.

It worked. The pounding boots thundered away in the opposite direction. He slowed, cautious, keeping to the empty back paths.

He ducked into a narrow alcove and pulled dried meat from the bag, chewing for much-needed energy. When the streets stayed quiet, he stepped out and turned a corner.

He ran into a wall of a man.

The man was massive, equal to Gorek's height, with hands built to crush steel. The stranger lifted him clean off the ground by the throat. Will's vision blurred as the air vanished from his lungs.

Will drove his thumb into the man's eye socket, deep and twisting hard. The grip loosened, just enough for Will to plant a boot against the man's thigh and kick free, dropping to the ground. He dragged in a ragged breath and rolled as he heard the mag-pistol bolt scorch past his ear.

Will grabbed one of his knives and hurled it with everything he had. It struck true, the thin steel sinking into the man's temple. The giant dropped instantly.

After pulling his knife, he ran, zigzagging through the streets toward the rendezvous location for the team. He knew he would not see the others, but Lydia should be waiting there. He finally slowed when no footsteps followed.

He braced himself against a wall, chest heaving, letting the rush of adrenaline taper. His hands shook. Blood soaked his white robe, most of it Angel's. He stripped the offending garment and shoved it into an overflowing refuse barrel. He was down to a single knife, the magical short sword from the vault, and his mag-pistol was likely low on charge.

With the last scraps of sunset fading, he looked toward the burning city. Only a distant glow remained. He pictured Chase and Connelly reaching the medics. He knew Angel would already be barking orders between pained breaths.

It felt like victory and defeat tangled together.

He thought of her face, and how she held his hand even while bleeding out.

If she survived… No. He knew she had. He would go back for her.

He would always go back.

He assumed she'd go to Media, but the truth hit him: he didn't know how he would find her without the Resistance. He would have to join them again.

By the time he reached the rendezvous point, nearly an hour had passed. The small town was quieter this far from the Order's alarms and the groaning fire-gutted buildings. He scanned the street and confirmed he was finally in the right place. It felt hollow without Dorna, Kell, and Angel. With any luck, Lydia would have given up on him and left. He contemplated killing her for what she did to that housing block.

The tavern's side yard stood empty, the dirt torn up by recent footsteps and hurried movement. He circled once, scanning the upper windows, then slipped into the adjoining courtyard.

That's where he found Lydia near an archway.

She was pinned against a stone wall, arms wrenched above her head by a man in ceremonial Order robes. For a split second, Will thought they were fucking. It wouldn't have surprised him.

Will closed the distance in complete silence.

As he neared, he heard Lydia's voice, low and purring. "Surely, we can come to some arrangement, love. You don't want to stain those pretty robes, do you?"

Then he noticed the rip in Lydia's dress, and the man's hand clamped around her neck. But her face told more of the truth. Eyes wide and bulging. Breath sharp and gasping.

He wasn't a guard. He was a high-ranking Acolyte, judging by the embroidery on his cuffs and the burnished silver staff resting against the wall nearby. He spoke to Lydia in a low, urgent tone. She laughed, brittle and mean.

The Acolyte's voice turned cold and predatory. "The Order doesn't negotiate with thieves." He lifted his mag-pistol, pressing the barrel against Lydia's jaw.

He should have allowed the man to save him the trouble, but he acted before he could think.

Will moved behind the Acolyte, grabbed his collar, reached around to his front, and drove his knife up beneath his ribs, right at the end of the breastbone. The blade met bone, then the tight, panicked clench of dying muscle.

The Acolyte gasped, dropped the gun, and twisted. His eyes found Will's, wide and full of terror. He tried to speak, but blood surged out instead, splattering his neck and collarbone in a sudden, ugly spray.

Lydia slipped from his weakened grasp as his body collapsed. She wiped the blood from her face with the back of her hand and stepped over the corpse without hesitation.

"Took you long enough," she muttered, sounding bored.

Will fought the urge to hit her. He should kill her on the spot, but Angel deserved someone better.

Would killing her make him better?

Instead, he grabbed her arm and dragged her beneath the crumbling archway.

"You set the fire to the housing block?" His voice was low and gravelly.

She rolled her eyes. "It was the perfect diversion. Drew three patrols away from the Citadel or more." She shrugged, as if mass murder were an inconvenient side effect. "You should be thanking me."

Will's fist clenched. He wanted to shout, to hit, but he forced himself to be still. Shoving her against the wall harder than he intended, he saw her pupils flare with something. At first, he thought it was fear. No. More likely excitement.

"There were kids in there," he said, through clenched teeth. "They never made it to the street."

Lydia smiled, and for a moment the cruelty in her was so naked it stunned him. "Don't play hero, Will. You weren't built for it."

He slammed his fist into the wall beside her.

He wanted to argue, but nothing came. He thought of Angel. Her blood on his hands. Her last order was to get the Tomes to safety at any cost.

He let Lydia go, stepped back, and wiped his blade clean on the Acolyte's fine robe.

Footsteps echoed down the alley, changing everything.

Lydia heard it, too. "Time to go," she chimed, voice bright and singsong.

Will didn't answer. He grabbed her by the wrist roughly and ran, dragging her behind him.

They ran through the night, and Will never dropped his guard.

He thought about Lydia and how easy it would be to cut her loose or cut her throat. Will wanted to leave her, but his newfound conscience refused to let him. He made a plan. One that would rid him of her for good.

When they finally reached a small inn far from the Order's patrol routes, toward Sarhan, Will allowed himself to relax.

He refused Lydia's advances, and she stormed off to the tavern to find sport after cleaning herself up.

Let her. Let her do anything... or anyone, as long as it wasn't him. He thought about his choices. About Angel. About Lydia. About who he wanted to be when the sun rose.

He hoped, for once, that the world would let him choose.

CHAPTER 12 –
PATH TO THE UNKNOWN

Will watched Lydia sleep in the gray pre-dawn, her naked back turned to him, a sheet tangled low around her hips. Her hair spilled across the pillow in a tangle of red, unruly and wild. In the low light, she looked smaller than he remembered. Maybe it was the way she curled inward, arms knotted beneath the pillow. Her freckles were visible even in the half-light, constellations scattered across her shoulder and nose.

A pang of guilt cut through him as he regretted accepting her drinks and letting himself get drunk in her presence. She had broken down his defenses and plied every seductive trick she owned.

He was scheduled to meet his Resistance contact this morning. Which meant he would be leaving her this morning. He should have been better than that, but thirty years of roguish habits didn't vanish in a handful of days.

Still, his thoughts moved to Angel. Drunk or not, shame sat heavy on his chest.

He pulled on his shirt, fingers moving slowly to avoid the snags where last night's buttons had torn free. The room felt suffocating, even by Sarhan's standards, with a window that leaked only enough sea air to keep the smell of sweat and candle wax from choking him. Outside, the port city was already waking with gulls, dockworkers, and the distant thump of footsteps throughout the inn and tavern. Somewhere, a bell chimed the hour. Five bells. He'd slept longer than intended.

He shoved the last of his kit into the enchanted bag... Kell's bag, the one that had allowed him to claim ownership. Its hungry mouth puckered shut with a metallic snap, swallowing most of his possessions in one go. He checked that the Tomes were still there, humming with the anxious static of unspent power.

He risked another look at Lydia. Her lips were parted, soft with a peace she'd never shown when awake. Last night's scratches trailed pink across his chest, and her bite mark still smarted on his collarbone. She'd been half-drunk, wholly relentless, her hands demanding and desperate when he finally gave in.

After days of telling her no, he had relented on the last night.

Will padded to the battered writing desk, opened the nearly dry inkwell, and pulled a blank page from the bottom drawer. He hesitated, pen hovering over the page, before scrawling a note. He kept it brief, knowing Lydia hated explanations. But he wrote anyway, fighting the urge to edit himself.

> *You deserve better than this. I'm sorry to do this, especially after last night. I hope you choose Aloria. The work there is safer, and you will be happier there than in this forsaken pirate town. If you stay, Zane, the barkeeper I introduced you to last*

night, will provide you with work until you decide to go. I've left you enough money for passage to anywhere. Use it however you choose. I've paid for the room for a month. No matter what, you will find adventure.

~W

He counted out coins from the magical bag, the weight of them almost offensive in the hush of the room, and placed them beside the note. Then he doubled the amount, just in case. Lydia's lifestyle was slightly nicer than that of a typical patron.

He slid the chair back with care, so as not to wake her. The urge to touch her one last time hit him like a punch. He resisted it. Instead, he moved to the door, paused, taking in the wreckage of the night: the overturned bottle, the torn curtain, the candle stub still flickering in its own wax puddle.

He gripped the doorknob, white-knuckled. The chill from the hall seeped through, making him shiver.

He looked back.

Lydia's hand had drifted across the bed, seeking him in her sleep. Her face was peaceful, but the lines around her mouth said she was dreaming of a fight. Maybe she always was.

He closed the door as quietly as he could, the latch clicking with the finality of a trigger.

The hallway outside was dark and unheated, the air alive with the shouts of kitchen staff and the sour tang of mop water. He followed the stairs down, one step at a time, until he reached the common room.

Zane stood behind the bar, as promised, cleaning tankards with a rag so filthy it looked like it could sprout legs and walk away. The massive tree of muscle he had known since childhood looked up at Will, expression unreadable, then nodded once.

"You're leaving? Wish we had more time to catch up. I'll make sure she has a place to stay and a job."

Will shrugged. "Didn't want to make a scene, and I have Resistance work to get to." He hadn't seen the man who was like a brother to him in years. Zane and his brother Corben had worked with him on trading ships for many years when they were younger.

Zane grunted and set the mug aside. "She'll be pissed."

"Better pissed than dead. She's no Felicity," he said, bringing up the woman Zane had helped him buy a ring for, before she disappeared.

The innkeeper looked away, wiping the counter. "I understand why, after meeting her last night. If you head back to Media, make sure Corben knows how much I miss my twin."

"I just might head back there. A lot is still up in the air."

Zane smirked, his eyes softening the smallest degree. "She ever figure out you're in love with someone else?"

Will's jaw flexed. He didn't answer.

Zane laughed as he wiped down the long wooden bar top. "Didn't think so." He poured a finger of clear liquor and slid it across the bar. "On the house. For luck."

Will knocked it back. The burn was nothing compared to what waited for him if he stayed. They exchanged a quick hug and a brief handshake, then he turned to leave without another word.

He left the bar, the inn, and Zane's silent commiseration. The dockside air hit him, sharp and wet, smelling of brine and diesel. Early morning was the only time moisture touched the air in the arid pirate town. The sky was bruised with morning, a smudge of orange over the rooftops.

He cut through the fish market, avoiding the main square, heading for the edge of the harbor. The stones underfoot were slick, and his boots echoed with a steadiness he didn't feel. He passed vendors setting up for the day. None gave him more than a glance.

He knew this city well after years of nefarious dealings. It felt different... emptier, or maybe just quieter inside his head.

He stopped halfway down a side street and leaned against the wall. He should have had the guts to tell her to her face, instead of leaving a note.

What would he say? He wasn't sure. That he'd miss her? That she'd been fun? Lies. He wouldn't miss her. She hadn't really been fun. Telling her the truth... That he hated her for what she'd done wouldn't change anything.

None of it would have mattered. She'd have wanted him to stay anyway, and he might have considered it... If not for the knowledge that Angel was out there waiting for him.

He closed his eyes. He remembered the curve of Angel's mouth when she smiled, the heat of her breath in the dark, and the way she said his name.

He pushed off the wall and kept walking.

The rendezvous was set for sunrise, three blocks from the harbor, at a lighthouse so decrepit even the city rats avoided it. Will followed the map in his mind. He checked every alley, every open door, and every blind corner for tails.

No one followed.

Dawn burned away the city's nighttime rot, leaving only the sharp salt of the tide and the grease of a hundred fires cooking breakfast. Sarhan's streets belonged to the fishermen this early, bodies stooped from a lifetime of hauling, boots sloshing through puddles of sea and offal. In the alleys, Will heard the crack and slap of knives against cutting boards, the hiss of oil, and the cursing of merchants haggling over what the day's catch was worth.

When the lighthouse entrance came into view, he paused. He didn't want anyone to know about the bag, so he removed the Tomes to carry them. The books pulsed, uneasy, as if they hated his touch. He tucked them under his arm and headed for the door.

Behind him, the city woke. The sky cleared. It was going to be a beautiful day.

It was a day of change.

He didn't look back.

The lighthouse was three stories tall if you counted the skeleton of what used to be the lantern housing. Paint flaked from the stone in ribbons, and the metal rails on the stairs were eaten through by rust and salt. It had the look of a place no one bothered to watch because it was already dead.

He stopped at the first step, felt the throb of the Tomes under his arm, and listened. Just the gulls and the slap of waves against the break wall. No voices. No footsteps. He climbed.

Inside, it was even colder; the air dense with the stink of rotting kelp and the faint copper tang of dried blood. The entrance chamber was empty except for a single, hooded magical lantern burning blue on a crate in the corner. Its light didn't reach the edges of the room.

A figure stood beside it, hands in pockets, face buried behind a mop of brown hair and a scarf wound high. They were not tall, with broad hips and thick arms. It was the kind of body that seemed to have grown armor against the world. Will couldn't guess the gender or the age; the city had a way of sanding those things down.

His hands drifted to his sheathed knives.

The figure saw the motion and nodded. "You're early." The voice was dry as gravel.

"Couldn't sleep," Will said.

His jaw worked at the pause, then added the first part of the passcode. "The tide brings strange gifts."

"Only for those who know where to look."

Will let himself breathe. The codes were correct.

They both waited, the ritual hanging in the air.

The figure appeared calm, almost bored, but tension sharpened their jaw, and their eyes never left his hands.

The figure's head tilted, just enough to make Will's skin crawl. "You brought it?"

He kept his distance as he set the wrapped bundle on the crate beside the lantern. "As agreed."

The figure reached for the Tomes, and unwrapped them with care. The books pulsed as they moved, a shimmer of angry red and black beneath the wrappings. The figure's gloved hand lingered on the covers a moment longer than necessary, as if listening for something only they could hear.

"These are dangerous," the figure said, tucking the Tomes into a battered satchel. "You read them?"

Will shook his head. "Not my style. I just deliver." He had tried, but he didn't know the language.

The figure grunted approval. "Good. Means you'll live longer. The last one who read them went mad, or so they say."

Will glanced around the chamber, noting every exit and every stack of crates that might conceal another body.

Something in the set of the figure's shoulders told him it was time to leave. Instead, he asked, "You'll get these to the right hands?"

"They're already in the right hands." The figure's voice softened slightly, as if sharing a secret. "The rest is just noise."

They reached into their coat and produced a banknote and a small burlap pouch that rattled with coins. With shaky hands, they held them out to him.

"Your payment. Standard plus half again for the risk."

He looked at the money, then at the figure's face. "I don't want it."

They blinked, nonplussed. "It's yours. Take it. You earned it."

He shook his head, his voice rough. "I did it for another purpose."

Their expression didn't soften, but they set the payment on the crate. "That's rare around here."

Will didn't let his face change, but he ventured a question pulling on his heart. "Is Angel alive?"

A flicker, then a shrug. "No. We don't know the details, but they were attacked on the way to extraction. The two she was with were captured, giving her time to get to the extraction point. Her wounds were too severe. She didn't make it. The extraction team couldn't save her."

Will swayed and folded his arm over his stomach. He hadn't expected that answer, but he didn't dare let this stranger see how deeply it hit him. He held himself together.

Silence settled, broken only by the wind slipping through the cracks in the wall. Finally, the figure straightened.

"You're done, Hawk. There's a boat in the east harbor. Name's Cutter. They'll take you wherever you want. They leave in twenty. Be on it, or don't. Your fees are already paid."

The figure gathered the Tomes, tucked them into the satchel, and slung it across their back. "Want a piece of advice?"

Will blinked, his world crashing around him. "Not particularly."

"Run. Don't look back."

He gave a soft laugh, raw and exhausted. "That's always the plan. Nobody ever sticks to it."

The figure nodded, not unkindly. "Maybe you're the exception."

Will doubted it, but he let the moment stand.

The figure extinguished the lantern, plunging the room into darkness except for the frail fingers of dawn creeping through the broken windows. "Good luck, Hawk."

He stood there a moment, waiting for something more, but the figure was already gone.

He stepped outside. The city was in full daylight now, sunlight bouncing off the waves and the hard angles of the buildings. He felt heavy, but also lonelier than he had in years. He staggered toward the east harbor. He had to get away. From the city. From Lydia. From the thoughts of Angel that clawed at him.

He pulled up the cowl across his face, stuffed his hands deep in his pockets, and made for the ship. He bit back tears he knew he couldn't release. He knew they would come when he was alone, when he could get lost in her memory.

He walked, taking time to memorize the sound of his own steps and the way the new day crawled into his bones.

He started the day hoping he would be heading to Angel, hoping there might be a future with her.

That hope was gone. He was alone, but alive.

Maybe that was enough. Either way, he owed it to Angel to be the man she deserved.

It was then that he decided to return to the Resistance and help transport people out of the city. It was what she would have wanted, and he was the best at it.

CHAPTER 13 – NEW NORMAL

Will notched the arrow and aimed at the large beast before him. Standing eighteen hands tall on all four legs and twice that if it rose to only two, they were gigantic. Their long fangs were only dwarfed by their long horns. Its thick coat of long hair would require an exact hit, but it could feed his large caravan for days. He hated to kill such a beautiful beast, but if it found their camp, it would easily go into a frenzy of hunger. As it was, Will was glad he was downwind.

It had been months since he had handed the Tomes to the courier and heard about Angel's death. He hadn't believed it until he heard the same from Gorek. They weren't sure if Chase or Connelly had spilled any Resistance secrets, much less his name, but he was on guard anyway.

The arrow flew straight, hitting it in the eye, and the creature fell with a seismic thud. He waited until the last throw of life before walking up to it. Upon reaching it, he touched his head, then the animal's body, giving thanks for its life.

The rain had thankfully stopped only moments before. He had been hunting for hours, and this was the first decent-sized prey he had found; he was miles away from the caravan. He would need help getting the animal to camp. He reached for his comm unit.

"Hawk to camp. Over?" he called.

All he heard was static. He made several other attempts, but nothing.

Something was wrong. It had to be. They would have responded by now. There were others protecting the caravan, one was Yelsi, the Elven warrior from Mellryn. He was strong and fast. He was also telepathic, so he tried to reach out with his mind. Still nothing.

He turned and headed back to camp at a quick pace, wishing he still had the short sword from the Tamris vault. He made the mistake of being seen with it in Resistance Headquarters in Aloria. Leadership had insisted on examining it. They had promised to return it to him when he got back to the city, but its slow-motion magic would have allowed him to get back to the camp faster.

As he neared camp, he noticed the dark smoke climbing in the sky and the pungent smell of burning flesh.

On the outskirts of camp, he found the body of Telmont, the weaselly cook with his perpetually grease-stained apron now soaked crimson. A black-fletched arrow protruded from between his shoulder blades, the shaft quivering slightly in the breeze. Telmont lay face down, fingers still clutching a wooden spoon, half-submerged in mud turned rusty with blood. The precision of the wound with a clean puncture through the ribs would have pierced his heart instantly. It spoke of either marksmanship or uncanny fortune.

Will crept forward, each footstep was deliberate and silent. Devastation was everywhere, and he scanned it through narrow eyes.

The camp lay in eerie stillness, save for the crackling of dying fires and the soft flutter of torn tents in the breeze. Bodies were strewn across the clearing like discarded dolls.

The trader Morrick had been killed protecting the twins from Westhollow, who were crumpled beside their mother's outstretched hand. A child's stuffed bear, one button eye missing, lay in a puddle of congealed blood next to the unmoving body of its owner.

It broke him.

His throat constricted painfully as hot tears blurred his vision, turning the carnage into watercolor smears of crimson and ash. His brain kept trying to piece together why anyone would slaughter an entire caravan for seemingly nothing.

The merchant's silks and spices lay scattered across blood-soaked earth, jeweled trinkets glinted dully in the fading light, and barrels of wine were split open to mix with the mud.

Will moved among the bodies, counting faces he'd shared meals with just hours before, memorizing each death mask. That was when a terrible suspicion took root, and he began methodically checking who might be missing from this tableau of butchery. He had found all but one.

Yelsi, but it couldn't have been him. He was an oathed warrior. He could not and would not have done this.

A movement caught the corner of his eye. On the outskirts of camp, tied to a wagon wheel with blood-crusted rope, was Yelsi. The Elf's once proud face was now bloody with swelling already starting in his right eye. Blood had dried in rivulets from his nose to his chin, cracking when he breathed. Where his fingernails should have been were raw, weeping beds of flesh. The stumps where his index and middle fingers had been severed oozed dark fluid into the dirt. A ceremonial dagger with the Order's insignia on its hilt protruded from his abdomen, the fabric of his tunic puckered around the wound and soaked through with a crimson stain that spread like spilled wine.

Will pressed two fingers to Yelsi's throat, feeling a faint, erratic pulse fluttering beneath clammy skin.

Yelsi's remaining eye fluttered open, revealing a sliver of amber iris clouded with pain. His cracked lips parted, each word a rasping whisper that seemed to cost him dearly. "The Order... left me... as messenger." A wet, rattling cough. "Three of them... white robes with black trim... showed me your likeness on parchment. I couldn't speak false... but wouldn't reveal what they wanted..." His fingers twitched toward Will's sleeve. "They're hunting you, Hawk... Said to tell you... the debt of the Tomes and... insult to Tamris would be paid in blood."

The Order had found him, just as he had feared. Will fumbled with his knife, sawing frantically at the ropes binding Yelsi to the wagon wheel. The hemp fibers frayed slowly beneath his blade. A flash of white at the periphery of his vision made his battle-honed instincts scream.

He pivoted and dropped to one knee, the knife still clutched in his white-knuckled grip. The Order Votary charged toward him, sunlight glinting off the blade raised high above the attacker's hood-shadowed face.

Will's knife found purchase between the attacker's ribs with a sickening crunch of cartilage. Warm blood gushed over his knuckles as he twisted the blade upward, then leveraged his shoulder against the man's torso to flip him overhead. The white-robed figure crashed into the dirt with a dull thud, limbs splaying like a broken toy, a death flower blooming on his chest.

A mag-pistol bolt sizzled past Will's ear, superheating the air with an acrid, electrical stench. Fifty yards away, two more Order Votaries advanced through the smoky haze, their white robes billowing around them like specters.

He sprinted for the charred remains of the supply wagon, boots slipping in mud and ash. The world slowed to the space between the crack of bullets and whip of arrows parting the air around his ears. Every muscle fiber in his body screamed in protest as he dove behind the spent axle, rolling through the belly of smoke that clung to the splintered wood.

Another crack of energy erupted from the Order's pistols, and a bolt burned a hole through the wagon's ruined canopy, showering him in a blizzard of wood pulp and embers.

Close. Too close.

The stink of burning canvas mixed with the coppery tang of blood made each breath a struggle not to vomit. He flattened himself into the shadow of the wheel, chest heaving, hands preparing for the next attack.

He scanned the periphery, heart hammering, trying to gauge how many assailants were out there. A second hooded figure circled to the left, moving to cut off his escape.

Will nocked an arrow, drew back, and loosed at the advancing pair. The first shot buried itself in the dirt. The second followed suit. His third found its mark, piercing one attacker's knee, causing him to lose his footing. The man crumpled with a howl.

His companion never broke stride, leveling his pistol as he ran. The next mag-bolt carved a fiery trench through the meat of Will's right shoulder, the flash-white agony so bright it nearly doubled him over. He bit down hard, tasting copper and smoke, and kept moving, dodging the next volley by pure animal instinct. His right arm went briefly numb, fingers spasming around the bowstring. Blood slicked his grip, but he forced the hand to obey, drawing back as the advancing assassin's hood slipped in the wind. A face as blank as ice, eyes void of anger or triumph, only calculation.

The assassin advanced with a pace so measured it seemed almost mocking, his dagger held at the ready with a surgeon's precision. Each footfall compacted ash and mud, never slowing. The assassin was five paces out, then three. Will dropped the useless bow and went for his knife. His hand barely closed around the hilt before the hooded man was on him, dagger flashing in a scything arc meant for his throat. The assassin's dagger sliced through the air, missing Will's face by a hair.

Far behind them, the world was still burning. The crackle of fire and the steady drum of Will's heartbeat obliterated all rational thought. He would not die here. Not after all he survived.

Will kicked upward, catching the man's knee. The assassin tumbled backward, not with surprise but with the mechanical smoothness of a dancer who had rehearsed this fall before. He rolled and came up again, not bothering to wipe the blood from his mouth where he'd bitten his own lip. The dagger gleamed; so did his eyes, cold and empty as a winter lake.

"Yield and I'll give you a clean death," the assassin said in a voice barely above a whisper. His accent was neutral, scrubbed of anything that could give away a home or allegiance.

Will spat, tasting the grit of his own molar as it rattled loose. "It is doubtful my death will be clean. How did you know it was me?" He assumed it came from Chase or Connelly, but it would be nice to hear the truth.

The assassin lunged, leading with the knife, a textbook killing stroke aimed for Will's heart. He sidestepped, feeling the blade graze his ribs, and locked his good arm around the man's wrist. The proximity was suffocating; Will could smell the faint citrus of the assassin's skin, the chemical tang of fresh bandages under his robes. The man twisted, driving his knee into Will's thigh, but Will didn't let go.

They circled, both breathing hard, though he had moved their fight to place the cart between them and the third Votary. Will's thoughts had narrowed to a single, red-hot thread: survive. The assassin's next strike was lower, aiming for the femoral artery. Will caught the descending wrist in both hands, fighting down the urge to scream as his burnt shoulder protested. The point of the dagger hovered an inch from his groin. He twisted the arm past its natural limits, heard the pop of a dislocating elbow, and slammed his forehead into the assassin's nose. Blood geysered over both of them, warm and immediate.

The assassin's eyes unfocused, his knife hand dropped a fraction of an inch as blood streamed from his shattered nose into his slack mouth. Will seized the moment, grabbing the man's dagger hand in a death grip and jamming his own knife up under the jaw, straight through the roof of the mouth. The assassin's eyes bulged with shock, then went glassy and still.

Will shoved the body away, hands slick with blood, chest heaving as if the whole world were a vacuum trying to suck the air from his lungs. He crumpled against the scorched remnants of the wagon, registering only now the fireworks of agony pulsing through his right shoulder and the hot, sticky shrapnel in his thigh. With a knife embedded to the hilt in his brain, the bastard still held on for a few last, grinding seconds, clawing at Will's shirt with the mindless, muscular insistence of a feral animal. The assassin's blood gushed, spattering Will's boots in dark, arterial arcs until the pulse gave up and the body slumped.

He staggered back, wiping his brow with the cleanest patch of sleeve he could find, and forced himself to look up, to scan for the third attacker.

Will ducked low behind the axle, senses tuned to every breath and shift in the battlefield. He risked a look around the wheel, blinking away stinging sweat and blood, and spotted a flicker in the haze of white robes, barely visible, ghosting between what was left of the collapsed tent and the burning skeleton of the merchant cart. He tried to steady his trembling hands, checked to see how much power was left in his sidearm, and left the useless bow where it lay, splintered and blood-wet.

He drew the pistol, cradling it left-handed as best he could, and braced his ruined shoulder against the side of the wagon. The next assassin moved with the silent, predatory patience of a snow leopard, weaving in and out of the smoke, never exposing more than a glimpse of pale skin or the faintest edge of a revolver muzzle. For a moment, the world seemed to slow, the crackle of fire and distant screams fading into a hush, just the oily whisper of the assassin's tread.

He wanted to call out, to taunt the killer into a mistake, but his throat was raw, and his mind was already busy drawing the angles of cover and sightlines. Instead, he sucked in a lungful of burnt air and waited, counting each step as the new shadow closed in from the left. The assassin was patient, methodical, always angling for a clear shot or a clean flank, never exposing his own body for longer than a heartbeat.

Will gambled on a feint. He tossed a chunk of wood over the axle, drawing a mag-bolt that sizzled past his ear and punched a smoking hole in the cask behind him. He marked the shooter's position. He had one move left, maybe two. He took them both.

Will lunged up and to the side, firing twice as he scrambled over the wagon's rim. One wild shot, one almost good enough. The assassin darted left, caught off guard by the suddenness, and that gave Will the extra half-second he needed to close the gap. He hit the ground in a tumble, rolled through a storm of cinders, and came up with the sidearm trained on the assassin's chest.

They stared at each other, both frozen, both bleeding and breathing hard. The Order man flinched first, going for his pistol. Will shot him in the sternum, then again in the neck for good measure. The body folded gracefully, like a dried flower, and slumped into the mud.

Will sagged to his knees, the pain in his shoulder now a roaring fire, and let the pistol clatter to the ground, as he noticed that these were mid-level Votaries. He had gotten lucky. If they had any more experience, he would be dead.

When he knew that they were all dead, he ran back to Yelsi to free him. The Elf hung limp against the wheel. Will used two fingers on his neck to check for a pulse. Nothing.

He released a roar of frustration that rivaled the beast he had slain earlier. He was dead.

Looking around the camp at the horror, he broke. Five children. Five children had been killed. If he were in camp when they attacked, all of these people would still be alive.

Why had they needed to die... Because this was his caravan? Because they were looking for him? Because they thought they were giving him a message through their deaths?

In total, there were twenty people in the caravan. All slaughtered to get to him. The Order of Tamris would not stop. This would not be the end. Anyone he was connected to would be in danger. He didn't know that they knew his real name, but there were enough who did. It was only a matter of time before they would find him.

He considered his options as he patched his injuries and prepared a fire. He didn't know the customs of Elves or the others to lay people to rest, but he would burn them to protect them from animals. They deserved so much more from him.

Hours later, the fire was blazing. These deaths added to his already large ledger. He wasn't sure he could ever get to black.

He gathered the supplies for the trip back to Media. The Order did not operate in Media, as Media equated all religion with magic, and Tamris was both. It felt like the coward's way out to hide from them, but until he had a better plan... he needed to go to the only place he would be safe.

Even if it was a city, he hated it.

Chapter 14 – New Life

Will sat on the low stool and let the smoke from the campfire curl into his face, half hoping it would mask the sting in his eyes that had nothing to do with wood or wind. It had been a year since he had passed off the Tomes of Moreth, when he had decided to start transporting civilians from Media to Aloria, something he was among the best at. He was headed back to Media to find other ways to help the Resistance. It was a chance encounter that led him to cross paths with his old friend Harmine on the road back from a particularly bad trip.

Harmine would have hated Lydia with her flame-red hair and caustic laugh. His wife, with her collection of pressed flowers and her soft-spoken ways, would have despised her even more.

Harmine hunched forward on the weathered stool, elbows braced on his knees, calloused hands busy with the old habit of turning a bone-handled jackknife over and over between his fingers. The movement was fluid, practiced. The blade caught the orange firelight as it spun, never once nicking the thumb that had lost its nail in the Sarhan raid.

He watched Harmine's hands for a long beat, noting how the scars on his knuckles had whitened with age before breaking the silence that hung between them like smoke.

"So I've made six trips and transported over fifty people out of Media since I handed over those Tomes. Things were going great until about three weeks ago. The Order of Tamris hit the caravan at dusk," Will said, voice so hoarse it barely carried over the wind. "Our caravan was two days out of Sarhan heading north. We put up camp while I was hunting for food and scouting ahead. The Disciples came from both sides of the ravine. They were as deadly as they come."

Harmine looked up, mouth tight. "Losses?"

"The whole caravan was slaughtered, and they tortured three to find me. They left one barely alive, just enough to send me a message before they died." Will drummed his fingers on his kneecap, a subtle nervous rhythm that didn't match the slow, steady pulse of the sea near camp.

Harmine waited, giving him space to finish the thought.

"I was only gone for a few hours, and they had three Resistance protectors. One was an Elven warrior."

Harmine's face didn't change, but his jaw worked side to side like he was chewing gristle. "You made it, though."

"Yeah. I did, but the twenty others, including five children, didn't." Will tried to smile, but it didn't hold. He knew the only reason the Order would have known his name was if Chase or Connelly had been tortured to give it. "It was horrific. That is why I'm giving up transporting. I'm not sure what the Resistance will have me do, but the

Order won't think to find me in Media, so that is where I go."

Harmine snorted, though his eyes stayed soft. "Pure evil to do the kids too?"

"Yep. It was tragic." Will spat into the fire. He flexed his hands and watched the heat eat the foam of his spit. "It's not going to get better, Harm." He shouldn't even stay here. "They will keep looking for me." He didn't want to risk the lives of people who mattered to him. He knew they would be targets.

Harmine gave him a lopsided grin. "Media won't be a bad option. At least your powers aren't obvious, like mine." Tiny sparks flew out of his fingers.

Will almost laughed, but the smoke burned too deeply for it to escape as anything but a cough.

"Yeah. I always wished I had cool powers like that. Being able to sense who has powers might be the only benefit. Maybe I'll find people who haven't been identified yet."

The howl of a wolfpack in the distant forest was thin and lost in the dark. The sound made Will flinch before he caught himself. He tried to focus on the fire, on the colorless tips of flame where driftwood burned hot and blue.

Harmine laid the knife down. "So, heading in tomorrow?"

Will looked away, let the silence fill with the snap and pop of pine. "That's my plan. Getting past their magic sensors isn't easy. Luckily, I know several other ways in. I'm wondering how long I can avoid Lysa and Gorek before they get mad. I don't want to risk the Order tying me to them."

Harmine blinked. He stared at Will, as if he'd just recited a line from a language no one else spoke. "Never thought I'd see you back in Media. If you had a choice, why didn't you go to Aloria?"

"Angel would have wanted me to help the people of Media get to a better life. She lived for it."

"Hopefully, it won't be for good. I know you don't care for the city. I don't blame you." Harmine said as he leaned back and let the firelight catch the whites of his eyes.

"I can only hope." Will hesitated, worried that he was lying to himself.

Would he be stuck in that city he hated?

"Married life is looking good on you. Ume must be treating you well. Or is that fatherhood?" He looked at his friend, noticing a glow about him.

Harmine nodded, a smile spreading, his eyes on the fire. "Without your help in saving my baby, I wouldn't even have my baby. Ume and me... we thank you for saving Emman from those slave traders. I don't know what we can ever do to repay you."

"I'm sure I'll think of something one of these days. Until then, I'm just glad your family is safe," Will added. "I don't have many friends, but I'm glad to call you one."

"I'm just glad I could do something to help."

He envied his friend's family, as he couldn't see a path to having one. He thought back to his parents and wished for a love like theirs. He had loved two women in his life. One had left him before he could propose because his life could be too dangerous, and then there was Angel, who had died because his life was too dangerous.

Maybe he was doomed to never settle down like Harmine. He could feel the scars on his body, the ache in his bones, but life went on.

He started to say something, then stopped. He poked at the fire with a stick, making the coals spit sparks.

"I'm tired, Harm. I haven't slept a full night in months. The worry that they will harm the people I love looking for me is eating me alive. I keep seeing the faces, especially those kids. Sometimes I think the Hounds of Tamris might really be God-blessed. They don't stop. I thought I was gifted in the art of killing until I went up against them."

Harmine took a while to answer. When he did, his voice was gentle, the way you'd speak to a wild dog caught in a snare. "You're not them, Will. You never were."

Will snorted. "Maybe that's the problem. Maybe I should be."

They sat in silence for a time, the only movement the lazy dance of the flame, the only sound the distant shuffle of the tide.

The night pressed in, cold and absolute, but the fire pushed back with a small circle of stubborn light.

They sat there, two conspirators, warming their hands and pretending it wasn't all going to end in blood. For a moment, the world outside the fire's circle didn't exist.

Will tipped his mug and let the liquor pool on his tongue before swallowing. "You ever think about what it'd be like, just to stop running?"

Just then, Ume called from the other room, causing Harmine to stand. He placed a hand on Will's shoulder, "There are forty guys out there on guard. No one saw you come in. You are safe tonight. Get some sleep, my friend." At that, he left the room.

Will watched the coals shift and flare, red to white to black again, and let himself imagine what it would be like to let the past burn down to nothing. That night, he closed his eyes, and for the first time in a long time, he didn't dream of the dead.

Be On The Look Out for...

Welcome to Aloria is Book 3 in the Series, where...

To steal items, an artifact, and a bomb from the Overlords in Fellspire Citadel, a near-impenetrable fortress. Once they steal the artifact, they must try to convince the Order of Tamris to trade it in exchange for not killing Will.

Will they need to fight the God Tamris for Will's freedom?

It turns out that Malin may be the prophecy Feniks Talavo or Phoenix Rising, according to the dragons. She will have to travel to Aloria to visit the libraries to discover the truth.

Caelum has decided he wants to get to know his daughter, but is he more than he seems? Where do his loyalties lie?

With both Malin and Anariel expecting babies, how will this affect life?

ABOUT THE AUTHOR

Brandy Stoker is a storyteller whose tales of love, resilience, and self-discovery captivate readers long after the final page. Growing up in Maryland, she draws inspiration from the charming landscapes and communities of her hometown to create relatable characters and vivid settings.

Brandy has been writing since middle school and is a proud mother of three adult children. Life challenges, including health scares and a difficult divorce, led her to embrace independence and inspire others to do the same. Her books reflect her passion for personal growth and the beauty of real-life connections, offering readers examples of resilience and self-discovery.

When she's not writing, Brandy enjoys coffee, watching koi, and playing games with friends. By day, she works in statistics and finance, balancing her analytical work with her creative side. Recently, she's embraced new hobbies like painting and caring for her koi pond.

Brandy invites you to explore her heartfelt stories and encourages you to leave a review. She loves hearing from readers and values their feedback.

Facebook, YouTube, and Instagram - brandystoker.author

Pinterest – brandystokerauthor

TikTok – brandystoker.auth

Her website is https://www.brandystoker.com

Check it out to find some hidden treasures related to these stories.

- Novellas
- Maps
- Character Art and more

Acknowledgements

The author would like to thank her family and friends for their encouragement over the years to follow her dreams and persevere in her pursuit of happiness. Without their gracious feedback and support, I would not have been able to complete this novel.

I want to thank my editor, Jennifer Windrow, for her efforts in helping me get this ready for publication. Her honest, experienced feedback enabled me to create this high-quality work.

I want to thank Angelee Van Allman for the Cover/Cover Art. Her designs embody the book's essence so well.

I want to thank Brandy Jones and Brandy Over 40 – Etsy shop for their art used in the Chapter Title art.

Most especially, I want to thank the readers. It means so much to me to hear from you. It was hearing from you that inspired this story. I hadn't written it, but at the reader's request and based on reader feedback, I decided to add it to the series. I really hope this meets your expectations.